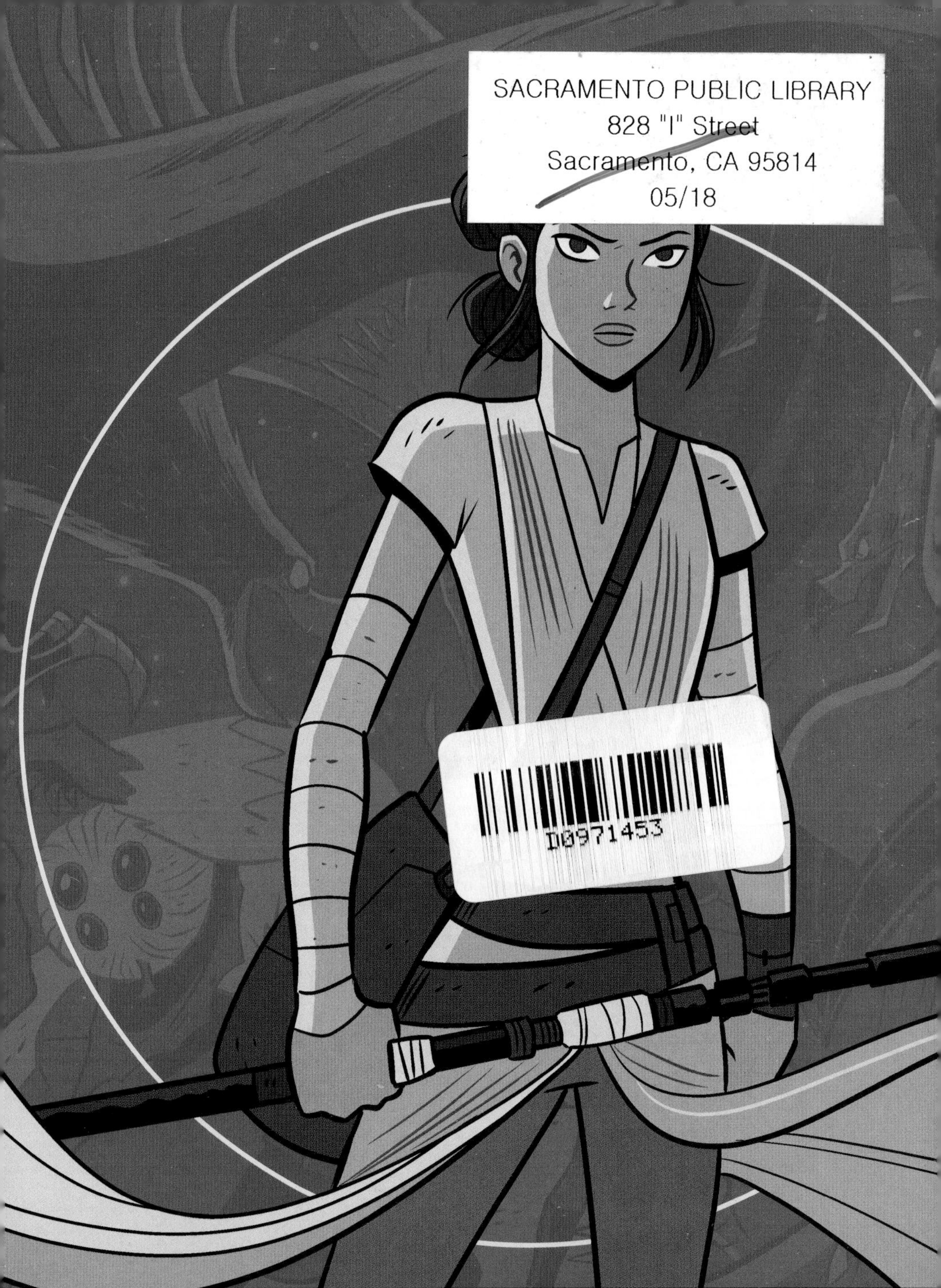

STAR WARS™ ADVENTURES

Facebook: **facebook.com/idwpublishing**
Twitter: **@idwpublishing**
YouTube: **youtube.com/idwpublishing**
Tumblr: **tumblr.idwpublishing.com**
Instagram: **instagram.com/idwpublishing**

ISBN: 978-1-68405-205-9   20 19 18 17   1 2 3 4

COVER
DEREK CHARM

SERIES ASSISTANT EDITOR
PETER ADRIAN BEHRAVESH

SERIES EDITORS
BOBBY CURNOW
and DENTON J. TIPTON

COLLECTION EDITORS
JUSTIN EISINGER
and ALONZO SIMON

COLLECTION DESIGNER
CLYDE GRAPA

PUBLISHER
TED ADAMS

Originally published as STAR WARS ADVENTURES ASHCAN and
STAR WARS ADVENTURES issues #1–2.

Ted Adams, CEO & Publisher

Greg Goldstein, President & COO

Robbie Robbins, EVP/Sr. Graphic Artist

Chris Ryall, Chief Creative Officer

David Hedgecock, Editor-in-Chief

Laurie Windrow, Senior VP of Sales & Marketing

Matthew Ruzicka, CPA, Chief Financial Officer

Lorelei Bunjes, VP of Digital Services

Jerry Bennington, VP of New Product Development

Lucasfilm Credits:

Frank Parisi, Senior Editor

Michael Siglain, Creative Director

James Waugh and Matt Martin, Story Group

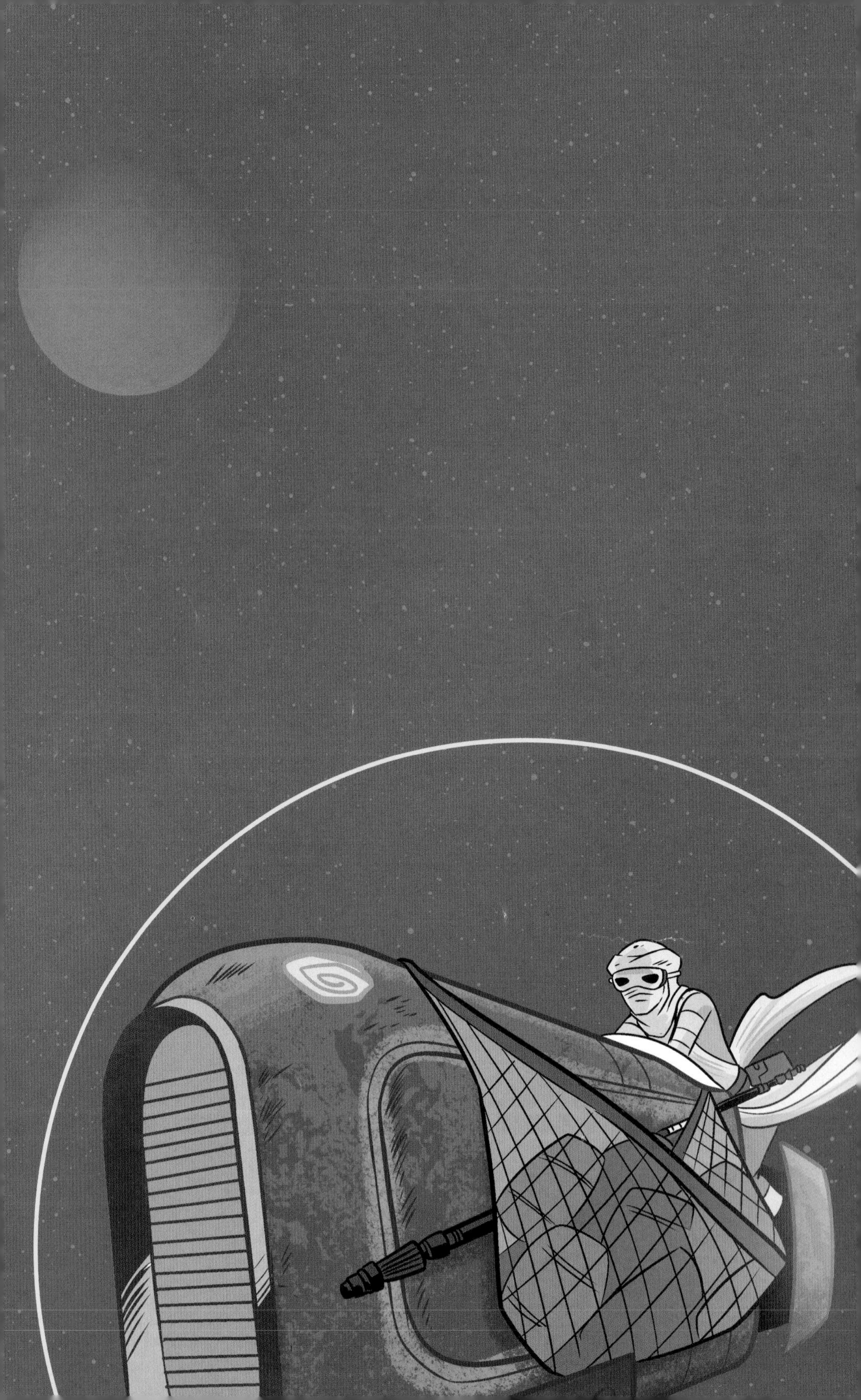

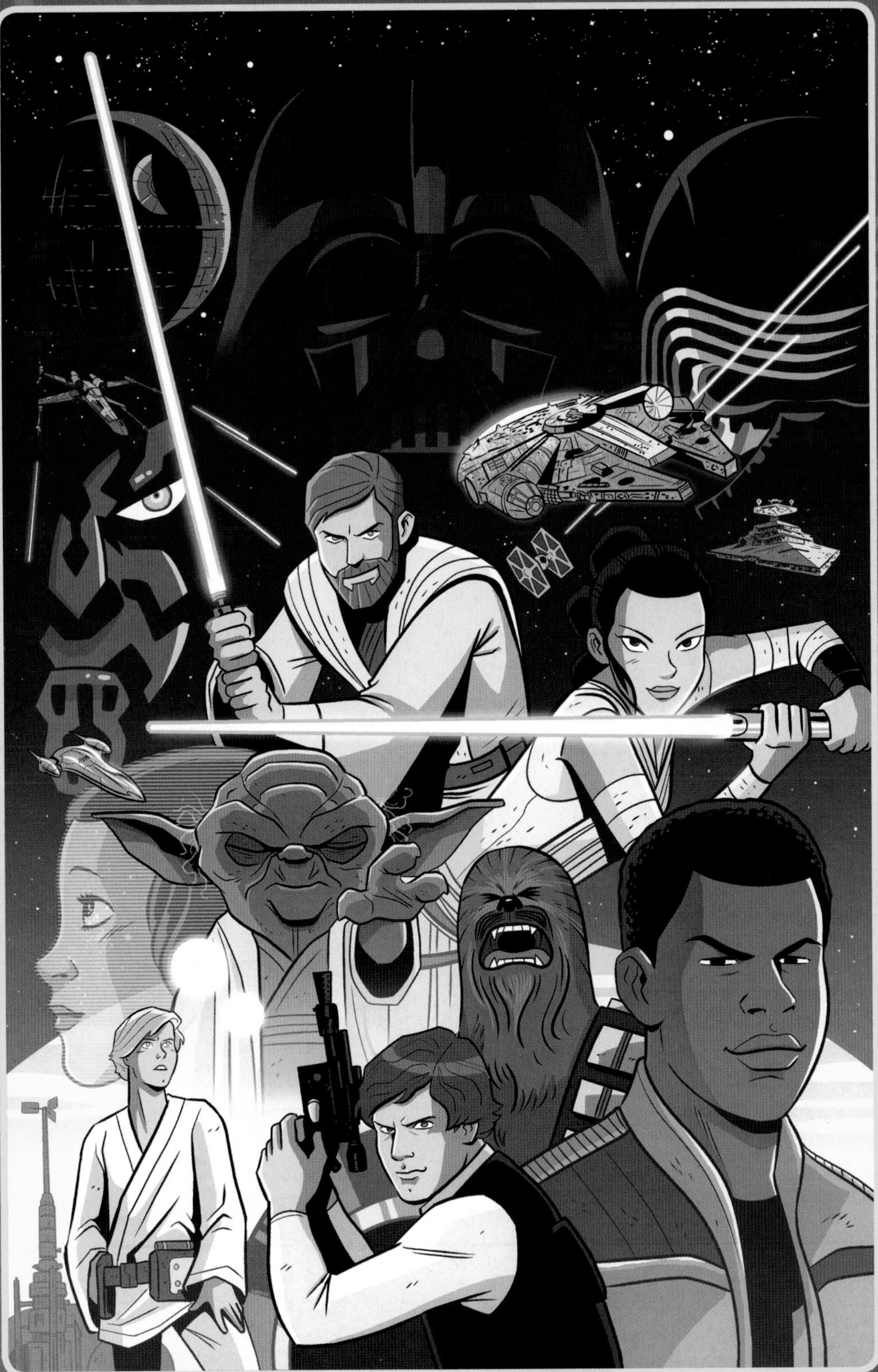

Art by Derek Charm

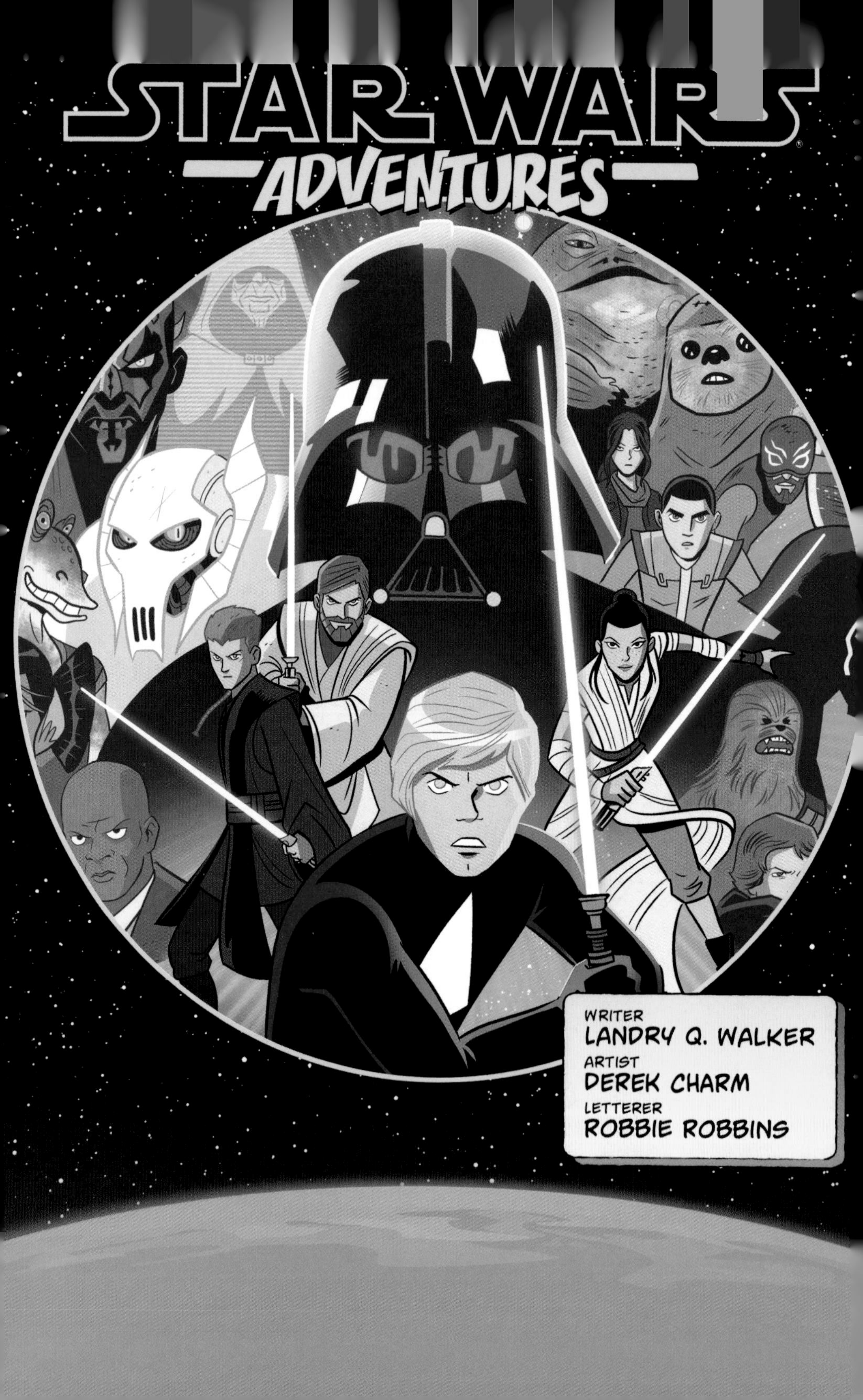
STAR WARS
ADVENTURES
WRITER
LANDRY Q. WALKER
ARTIST
DEREK CHARM
LETTERER
ROBBIE ROBBINS

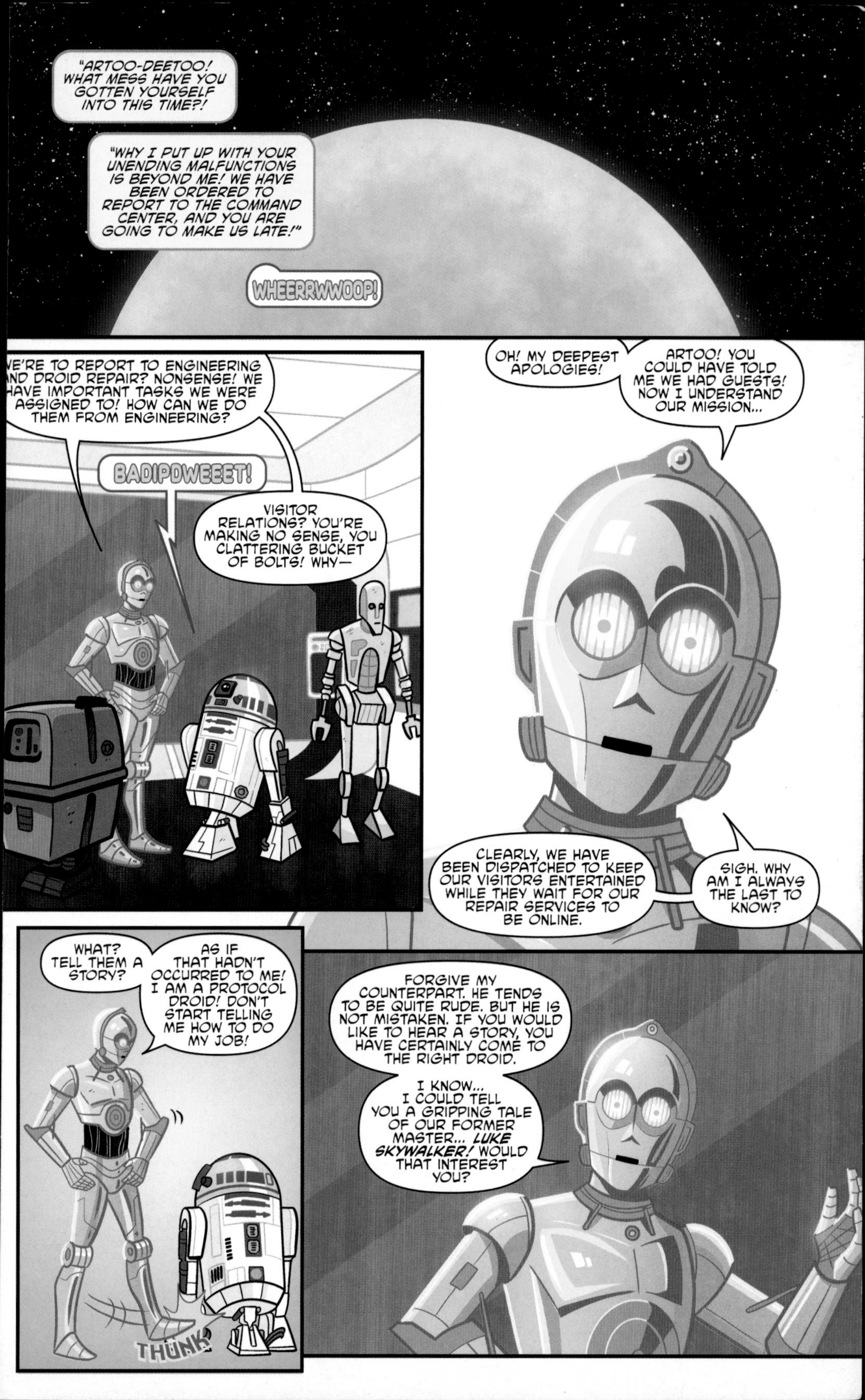

"ARTOO-DEETOO! WHAT MESS HAVE YOU GOTTEN YOURSELF INTO THIS TIME?!
"WHY I PUT UP WITH YOUR UNENDING MALFUNCTIONS IS BEYOND ME! WE HAVE BEEN ORDERED TO REPORT TO THE COMMAND CENTER, AND YOU ARE GOING TO MAKE US LATE!"
WHEERRWWOOP!
E'RE TO REPORT TO ENGINEERING ND DROID REPAIR? NONSENSE! WE HAVE IMPORTANT TASKS WE WERE ASSIGNED TO! HOW CAN WE DO THEM FROM ENGINEERING?
BADIPDWEEET!
VISITOR RELATIONS? YOU'RE MAKING NO SENSE, YOU CLATTERING BUCKET OF BOLTS! WHY—
OH! MY DEEPEST APOLOGIES!
ARTOO! YOU COULD HAVE TOLD ME WE HAD GUESTS! NOW I UNDERSTAND OUR MISSION...
CLEARLY, WE HAVE BEEN DISPATCHED TO KEEP OUR VISITORS ENTERTAINED WHILE THEY WAIT FOR OUR REPAIR SERVICES TO BE ONLINE.
SIGH. WHY AM I ALWAYS THE LAST TO KNOW?
WHAT? TELL THEM A STORY?
AS IF THAT HADN'T OCCURRED TO ME! I AM A PROTOCOL DROID! DON'T START TELLING ME HOW TO DO MY JOB!
THUNK!
FORGIVE MY COUNTERPART. HE TENDS TO BE QUITE RUDE. BUT HE IS NOT MISTAKEN. IF YOU WOULD LIKE TO HEAR A STORY, YOU HAVE CERTAINLY COME TO THE RIGHT DROID.
I KNOW... I COULD TELL YOU A GRIPPING TALE OF OUR FORMER MASTER... LUKE SKYWALKER! WOULD THAT INTEREST YOU?

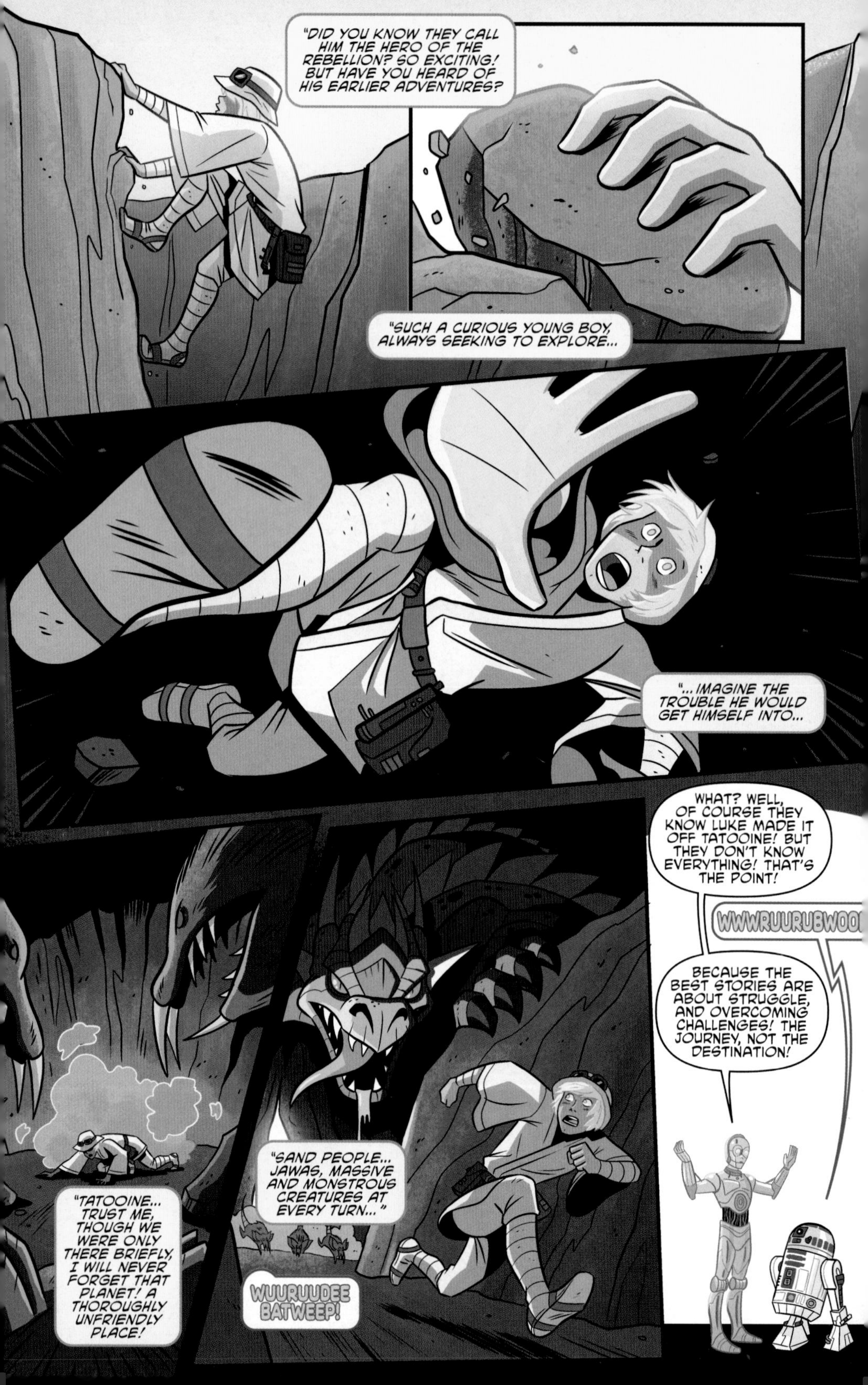
"DID YOU KNOW THEY CALL HIM THE HERO OF THE REBELLION? SO EXCITING! BUT HAVE YOU HEARD OF HIS EARLIER ADVENTURES?
"SUCH A CURIOUS YOUNG BOY, ALWAYS SEEKING TO EXPLORE...
"...IMAGINE THE TROUBLE HE WOULD GET HIMSELF INTO...
"TATOOINE... TRUST ME, THOUGH WE WERE ONLY THERE BRIEFLY, I WILL NEVER FORGET THAT PLANET! A THOROUGHLY UNFRIENDLY PLACE!
"SAND PEOPLE... JAWAS, MASSIVE AND MONSTROUS CREATURES AT EVERY TURN..."
WUURUUDEE BATWEEP!
WHAT? WELL, OF COURSE THEY KNOW LUKE MADE IT OFF TATOOINE! BUT THEY DON'T KNOW EVERYTHING! THAT'S THE POINT!
WWWRUURUBWOO
BECAUSE THE BEST STORIES ARE ABOUT STRUGGLE, AND OVERCOMING CHALLENGES! THE JOURNEY, NOT THE DESTINATION!

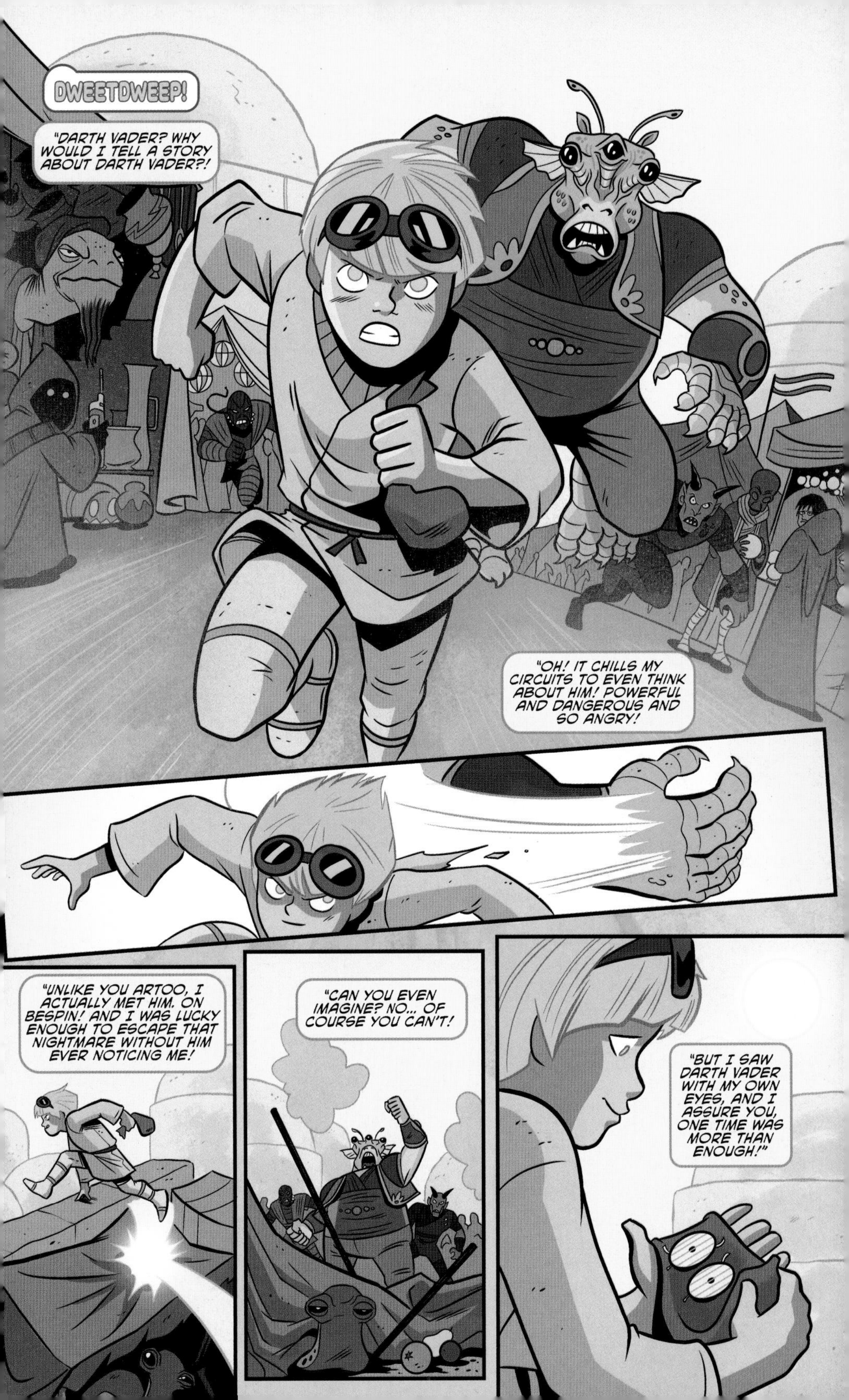
DWEETDWEEP!
"DARTH VADER? WHY WOULD I TELL A STORY ABOUT DARTH VADER?!
"OH! IT CHILLS MY CIRCUITS TO EVEN THINK ABOUT HIM! POWERFUL AND DANGEROUS AND SO ANGRY!
"UNLIKE YOU ARTOO, I ACTUALLY MET HIM. ON BESPIN! AND I WAS LUCKY ENOUGH TO ESCAPE THAT NIGHTMARE WITHOUT HIM EVER NOTICING ME!
"CAN YOU EVEN IMAGINE? NO... OF COURSE YOU CAN'T!
"BUT I SAW DARTH VADER WITH MY OWN EYES, AND I ASSURE YOU, ONE TIME WAS MORE THAN ENOUGH!"

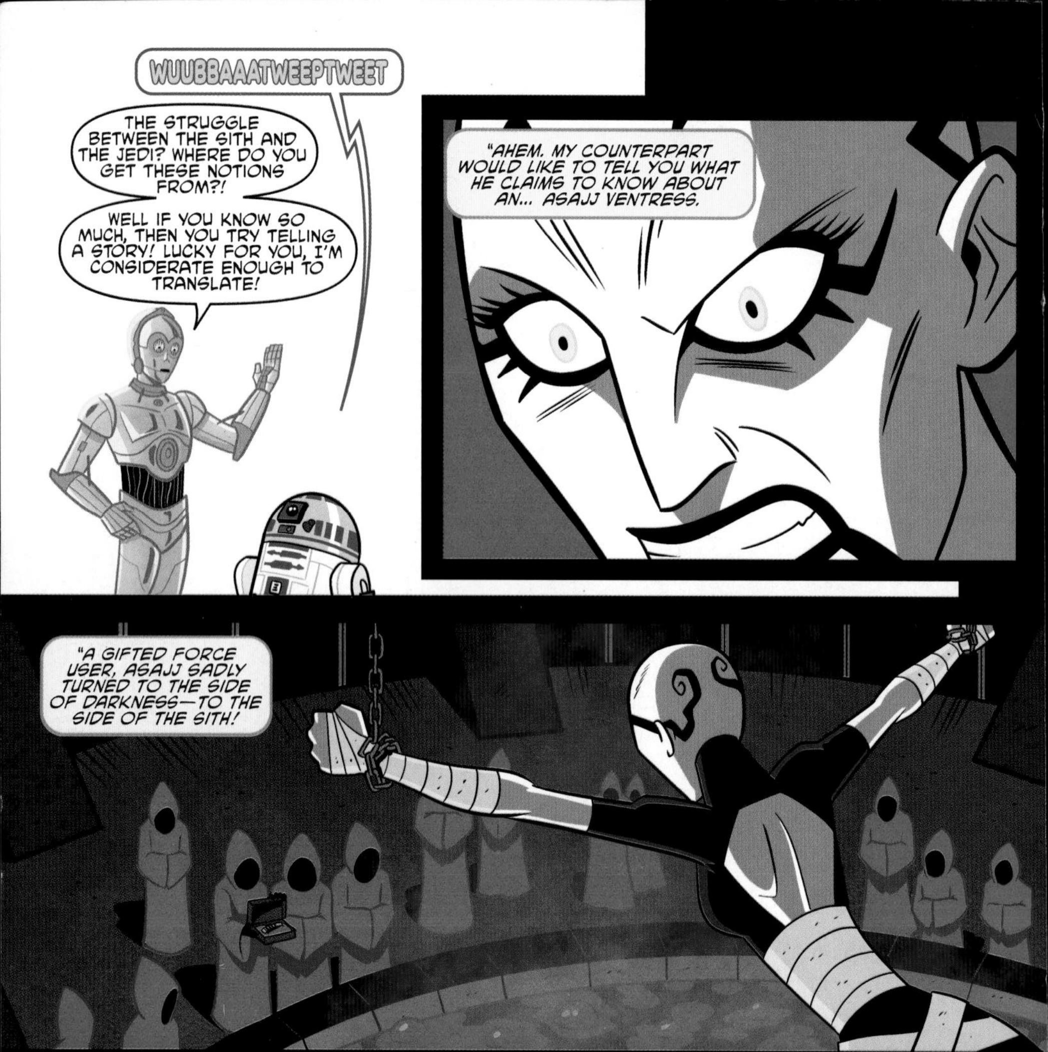
WUUBBAAATWEEPTWEET
THE STRUGGLE BETWEEN THE SITH AND THE JEDI? WHERE DO YOU GET THESE NOTIONS FROM?!
WELL IF YOU KNOW SO MUCH, THEN YOU TRY TELLING A STORY! LUCKY FOR YOU, I'M CONSIDERATE ENOUGH TO TRANSLATE!
"AHEM. MY COUNTERPART WOULD LIKE TO TELL YOU WHAT HE CLAIMS TO KNOW ABOUT AN... ASAJJ VENTRESS.
"A GIFTED FORCE USER, ASAJJ SADLY TURNED TO THE SIDE OF DARKNESS—TO THE SIDE OF THE SITH!

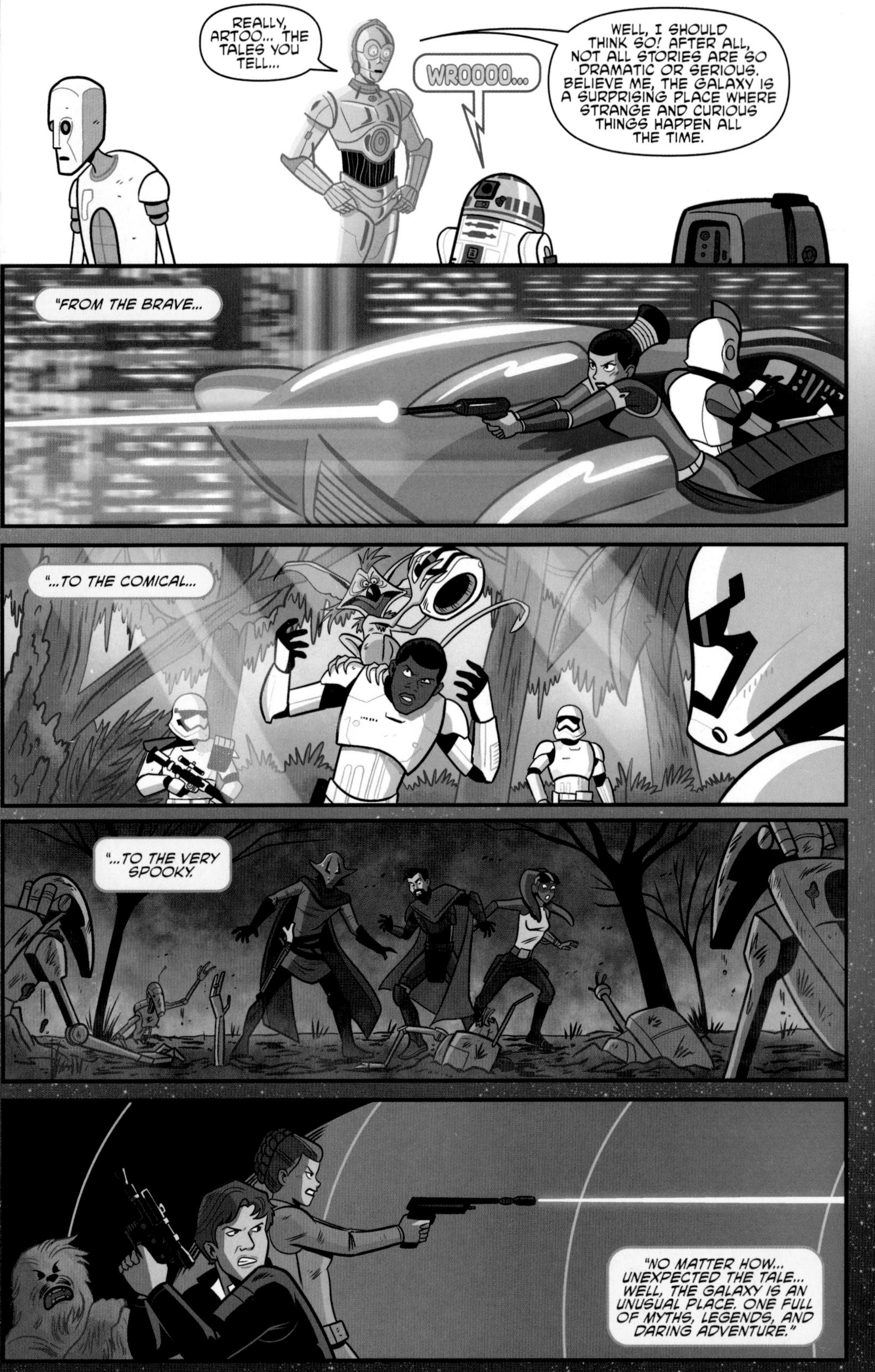
REALLY, ARTOO... THE TALES YOU TELL...
WROOOO...
WELL, I SHOULD THINK SO! AFTER ALL, NOT ALL STORIES ARE SO DRAMATIC OR SERIOUS. BELIEVE ME, THE GALAXY IS A SURPRISING PLACE WHERE STRANGE AND CURIOUS THINGS HAPPEN ALL THE TIME.
"FROM THE BRAVE...
"...TO THE COMICAL...
"...TO THE VERY SPOOKY.
"NO MATTER HOW... UNEXPECTED THE TALE... WELL, THE GALAXY IS AN UNUSUAL PLACE. ONE FULL OF MYTHS, LEGENDS, AND DARING ADVENTURE."

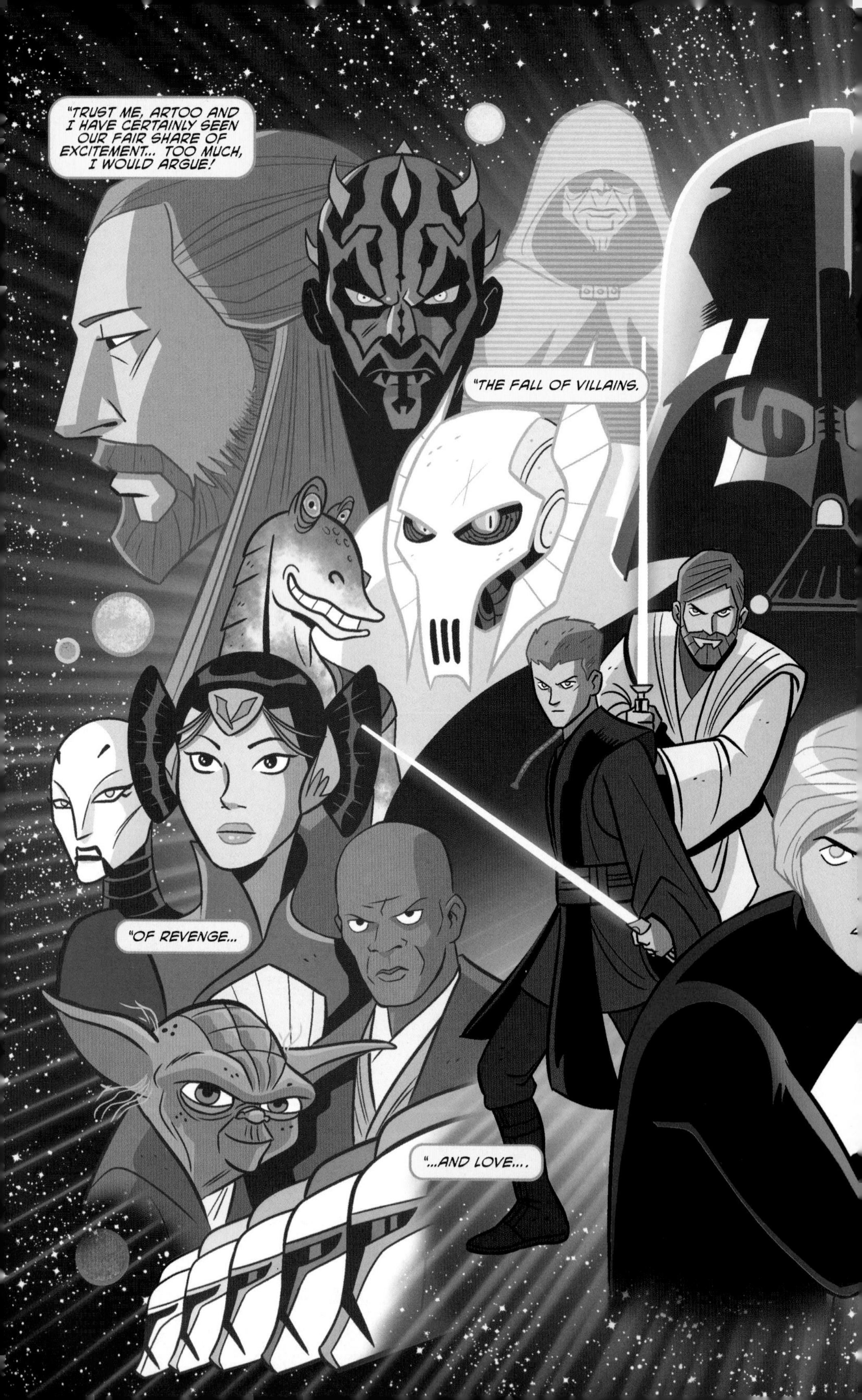
"TRUST ME, ARTOO AND I HAVE CERTAINLY SEEN OUR FAIR SHARE OF EXCITEMENT... TOO MUCH, I WOULD ARGUE!
"THE FALL OF VILLAINS.
"OF REVENGE...
"...AND LOVE....

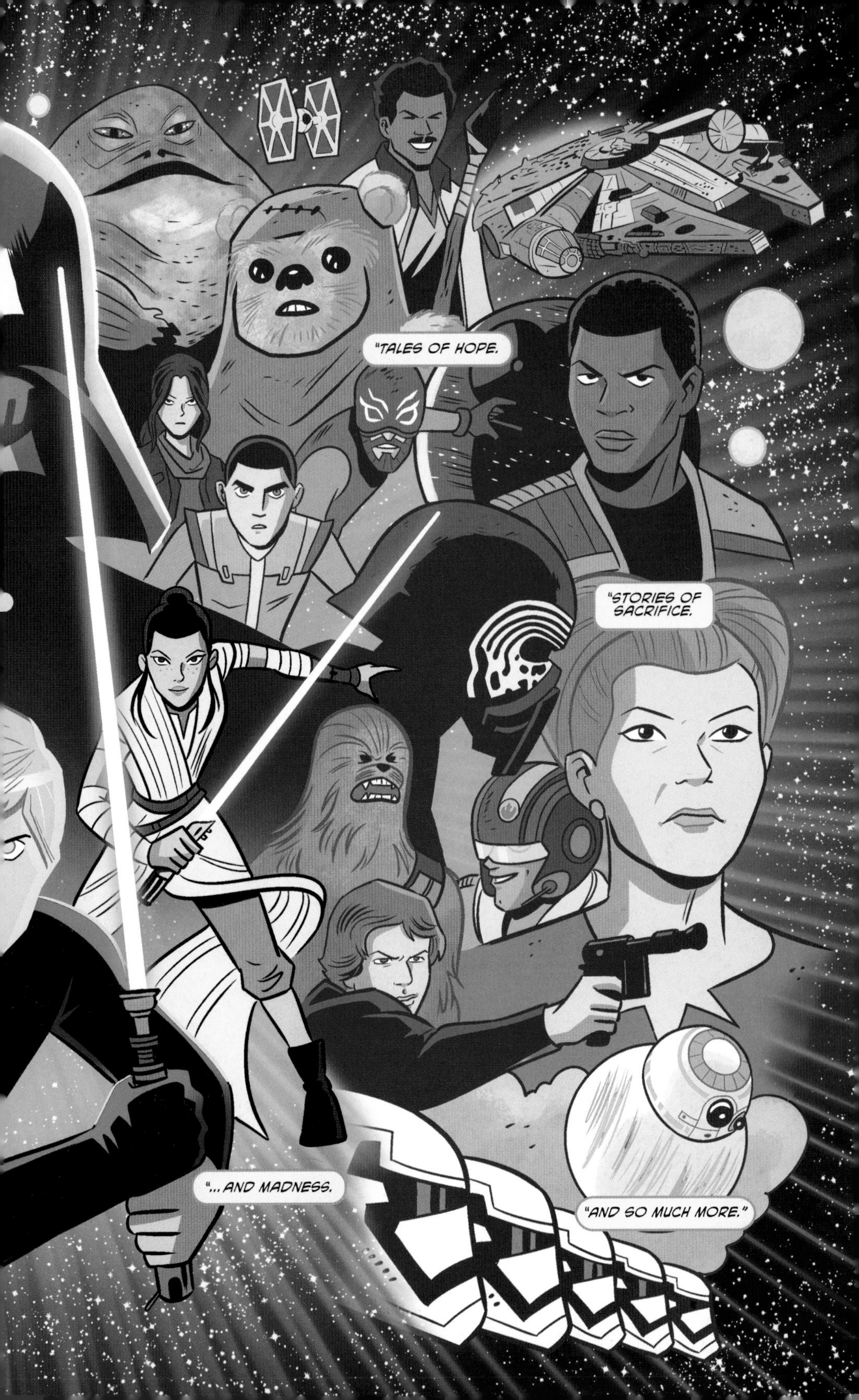
"TALES OF HOPE.
"STORIES OF SACRIFICE.
"... AND MADNESS.
"AND SO MUCH MORE."

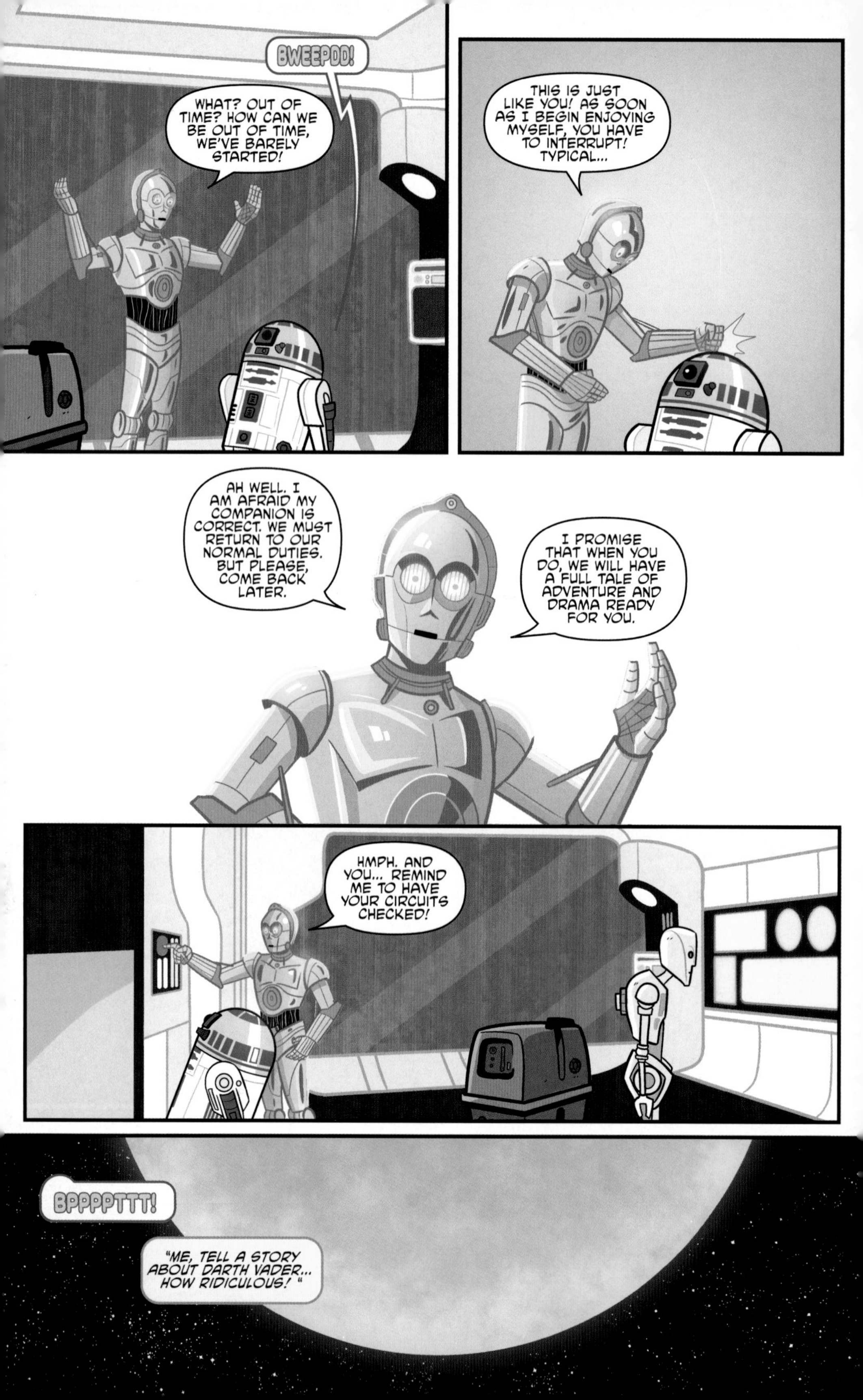
BWEEPDD!
WHAT? OUT OF TIME? HOW CAN WE BE OUT OF TIME, WE'VE BARELY STARTED!
THIS IS JUST LIKE YOU! AS SOON AS I BEGIN ENJOYING MYSELF, YOU HAVE TO INTERRUPT! TYPICAL...
AH WELL. I AM AFRAID MY COMPANION IS CORRECT. WE MUST RETURN TO OUR NORMAL DUTIES. BUT PLEASE, COME BACK LATER.
I PROMISE THAT WHEN YOU DO, WE WILL HAVE A FULL TALE OF ADVENTURE AND DRAMA READY FOR YOU.
HMPH. AND YOU... REMIND ME TO HAVE YOUR CIRCUITS CHECKED!
BPPPPTTT!
"ME, TELL A STORY ABOUT DARTH VADER... HOW RIDICULOUS!"

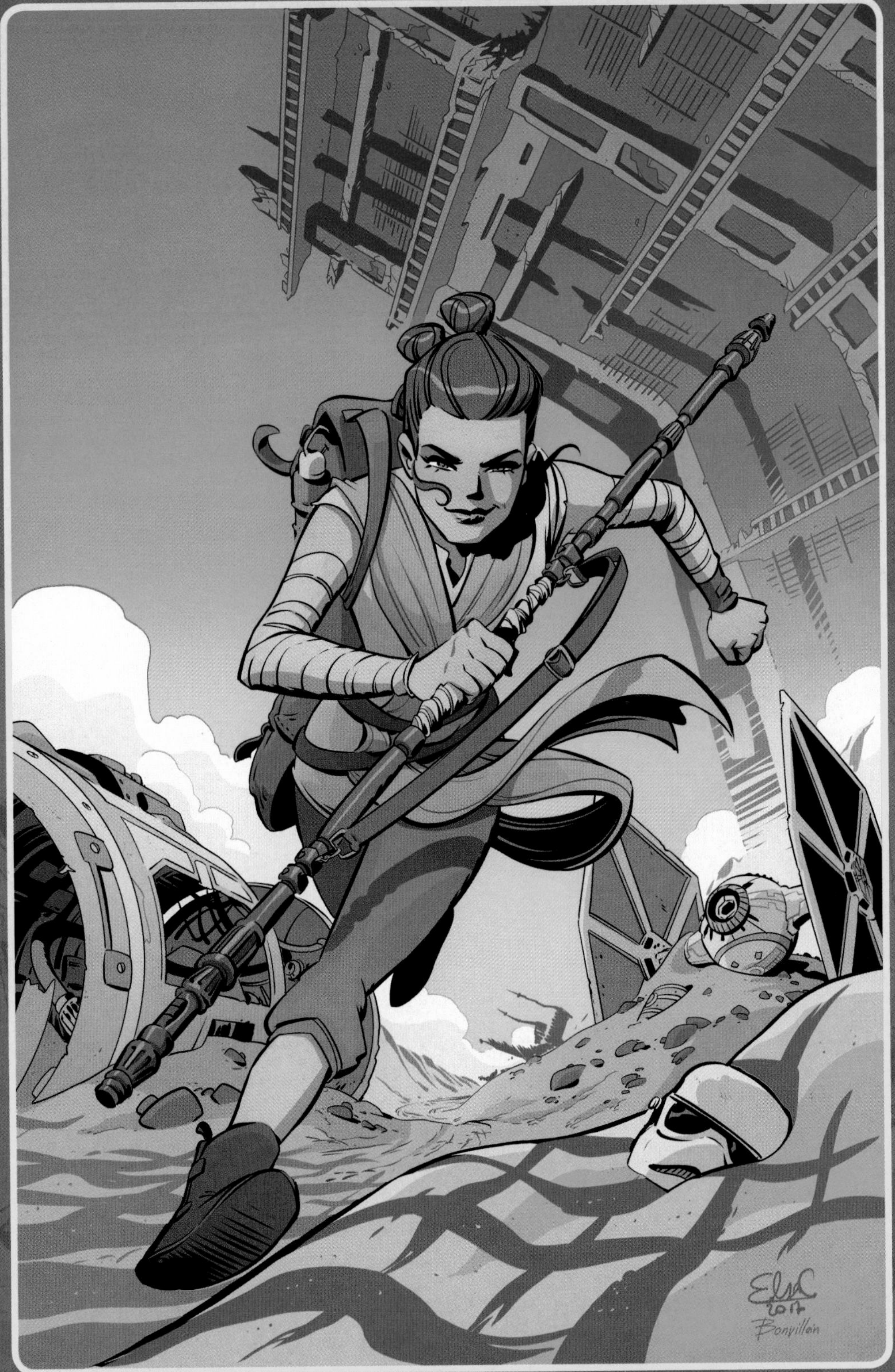
Elsa 2017
Bonvillain

Art by Elsa Charretier, Colors by Tamra Bonvillain

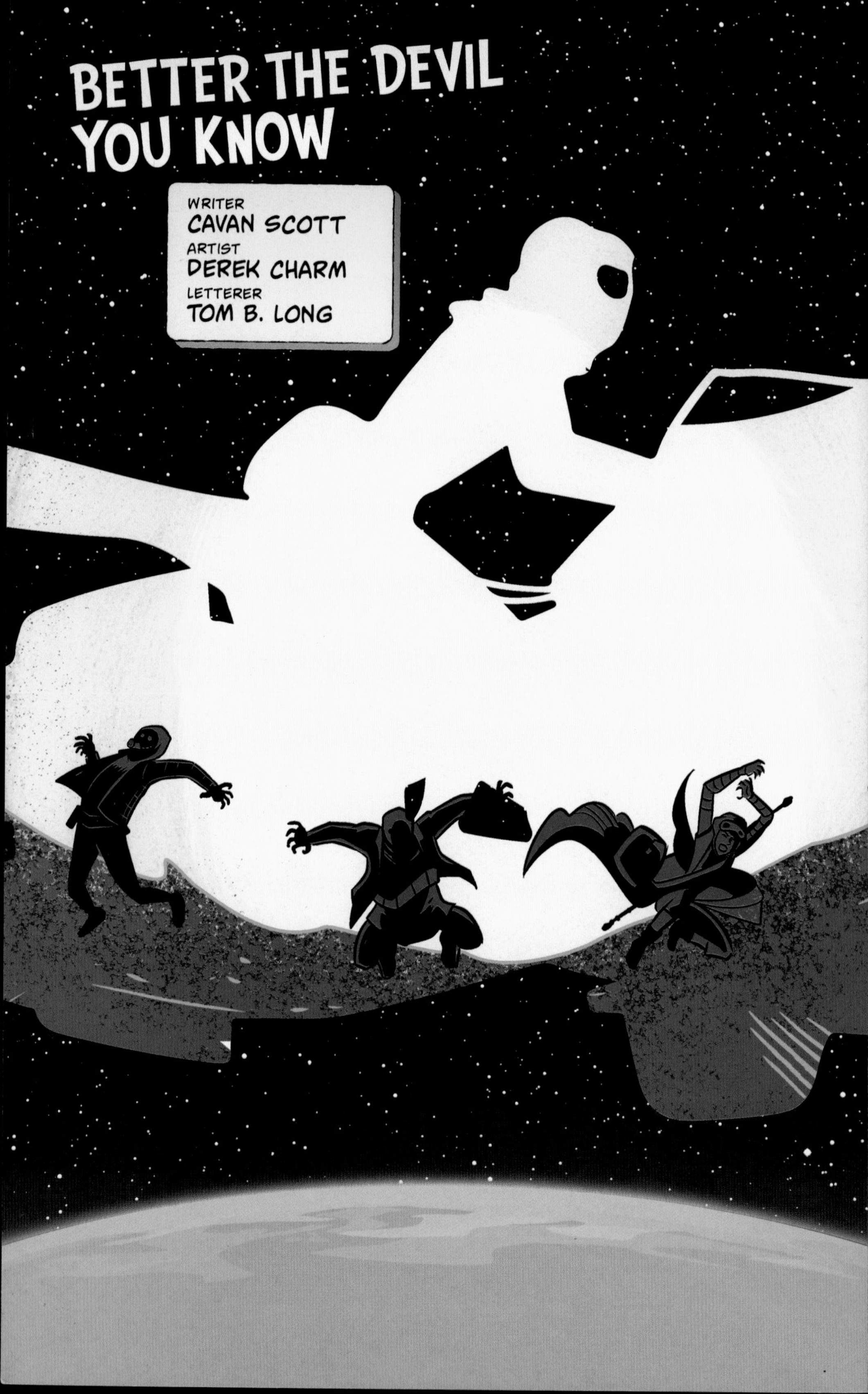
BETTER THE DEVIL YOU KNOW
WRITER
CAVAN SCOTT
ARTIST
DEREK CHARM
LETTERER
TOM B. LONG

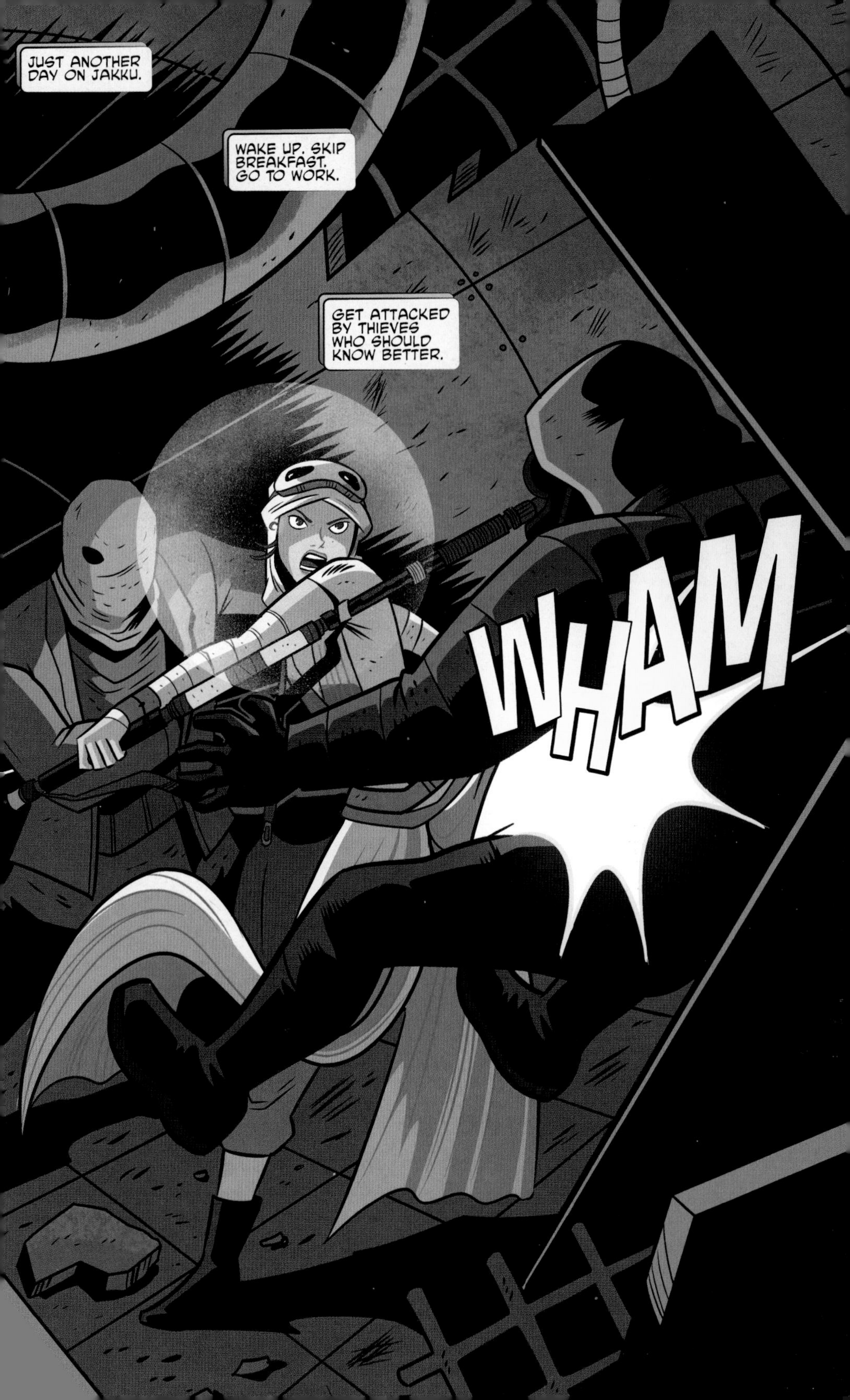
JUST ANOTHER DAY ON JAKKU.
WAKE UP. SKIP BREAKFAST. GO TO WORK.
GET ATTACKED BY THIEVES WHO SHOULD KNOW BETTER.
WHAM

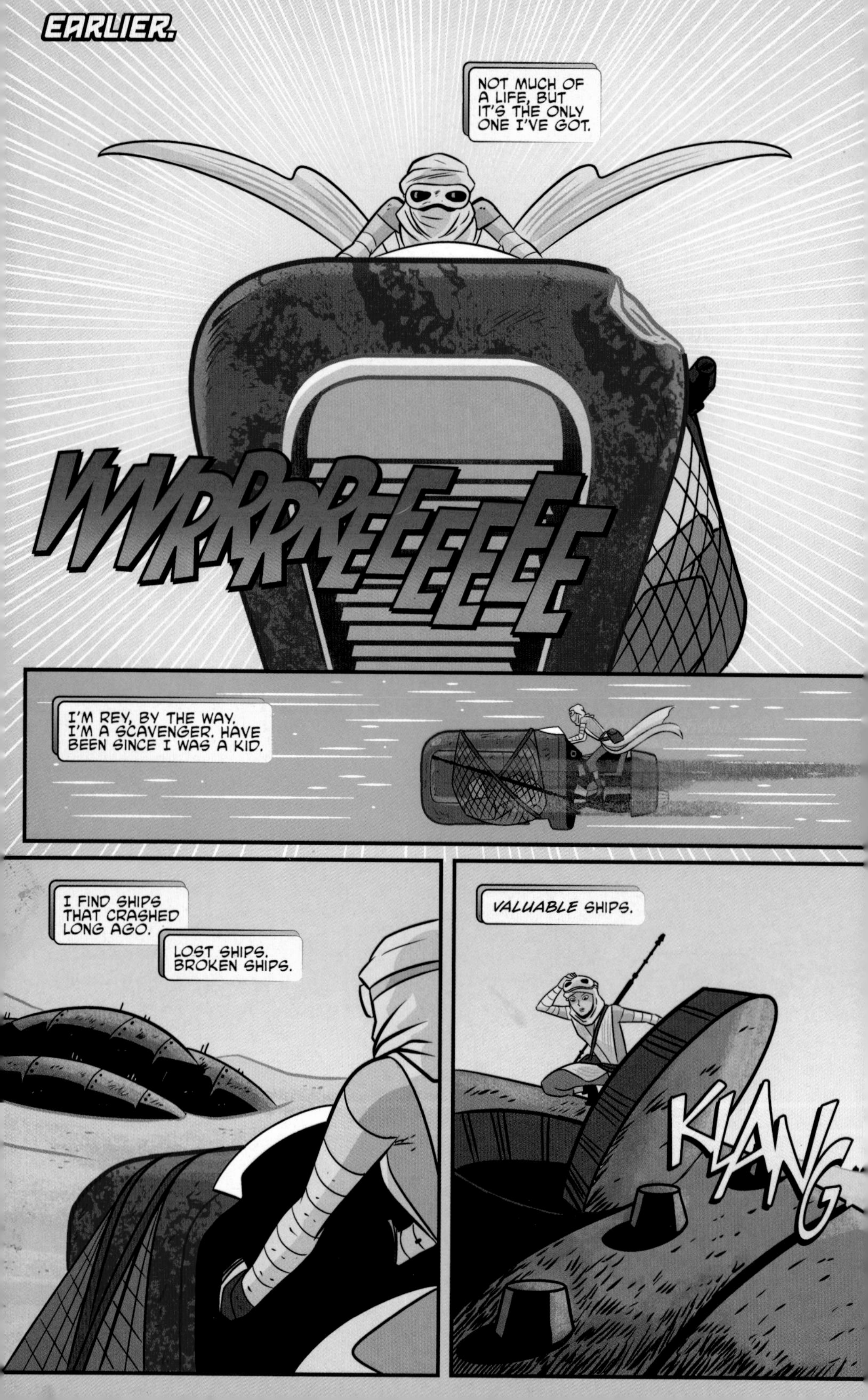
EARLIER.
NOT MUCH OF A LIFE, BUT IT'S THE ONLY ONE I'VE GOT.
VVVRRRREEEEEE
I'M REY, BY THE WAY. I'M A SCAVENGER. HAVE BEEN SINCE I WAS A KID.
I FIND SHIPS THAT CRASHED LONG AGO.
LOST SHIPS. BROKEN SHIPS.
VALUABLE SHIPS.
KLANG

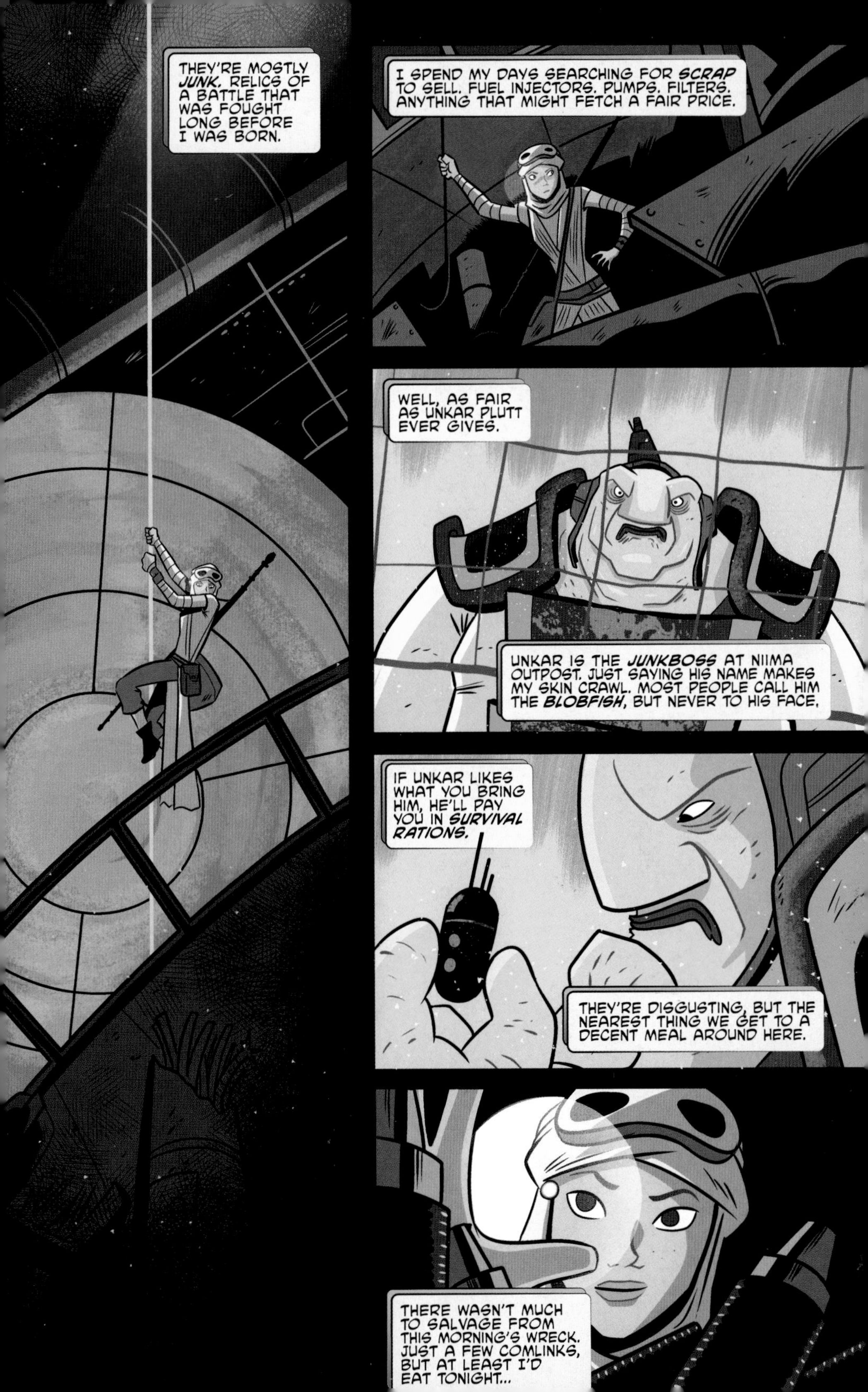
THEY'RE MOSTLY JUNK. RELICS OF A BATTLE THAT WAS FOUGHT LONG BEFORE I WAS BORN.
I SPEND MY DAYS SEARCHING FOR SCRAP TO SELL. FUEL INJECTORS. PUMPS. FILTERS. ANYTHING THAT MIGHT FETCH A FAIR PRICE.
WELL, AS FAIR AS UNKAR PLUTT EVER GIVES.
UNKAR IS THE JUNKBOSS AT NIIMA OUTPOST. JUST SAYING HIS NAME MAKES MY SKIN CRAWL. MOST PEOPLE CALL HIM THE BLOBFISH, BUT NEVER TO HIS FACE.
IF UNKAR LIKES WHAT YOU BRING HIM, HE'LL PAY YOU IN SURVIVAL RATIONS.
THEY'RE DISGUSTING, BUT THE NEAREST THING WE GET TO A DECENT MEAL AROUND HERE.
THERE WASN'T MUCH TO SALVAGE FROM THIS MORNING'S WRECK. JUST A FEW COMLINKS, BUT AT LEAST I'D EAT TONIGHT...

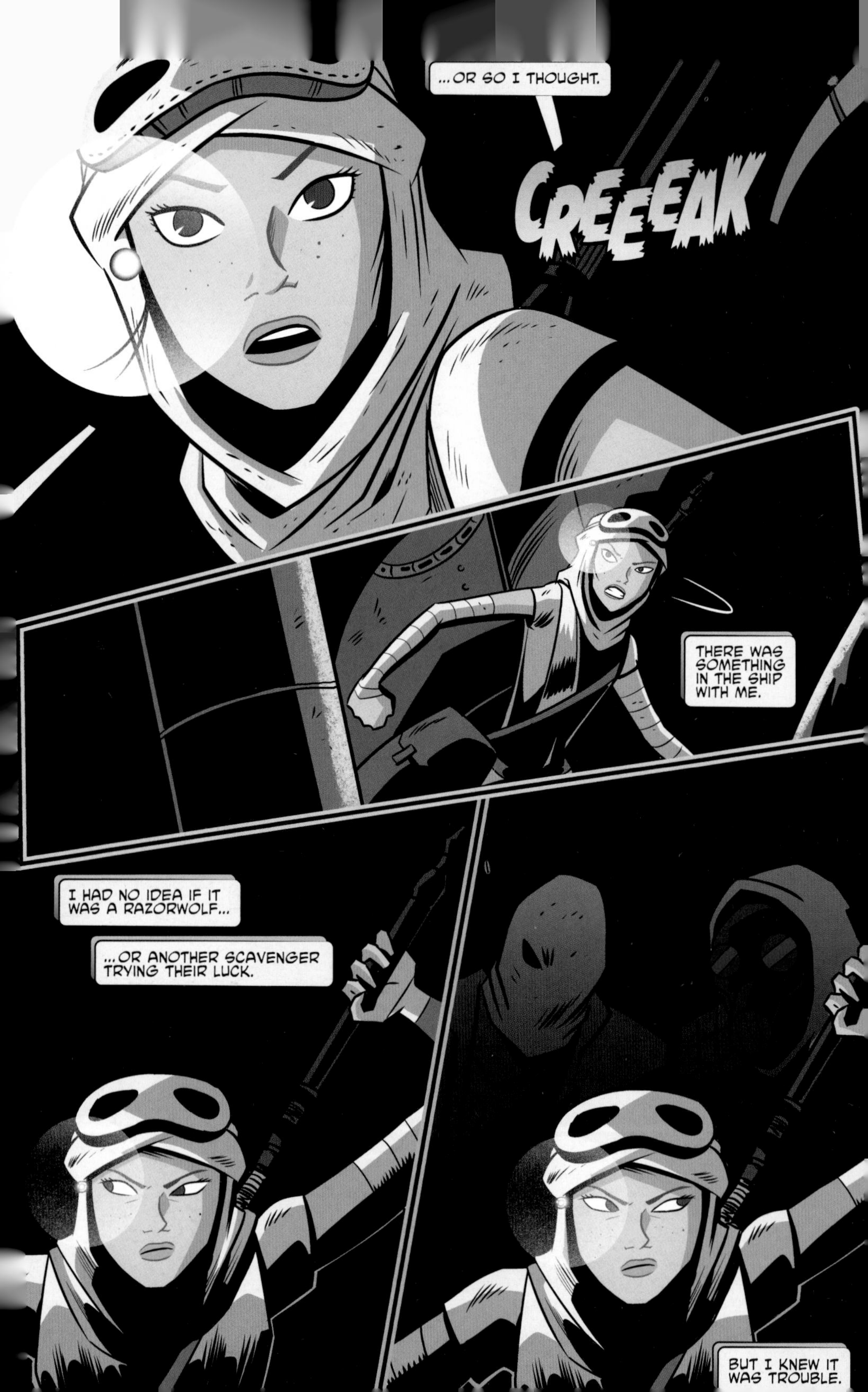
...OR SO I THOUGHT.
CREEEAK
THERE WAS SOMETHING IN THE SHIP WITH ME.
I HAD NO IDEA IF IT WAS A RAZORWOLF...
...OR ANOTHER SCAVENGER TRYING THEIR LUCK.
BUT I KNEW IT WAS TROUBLE.

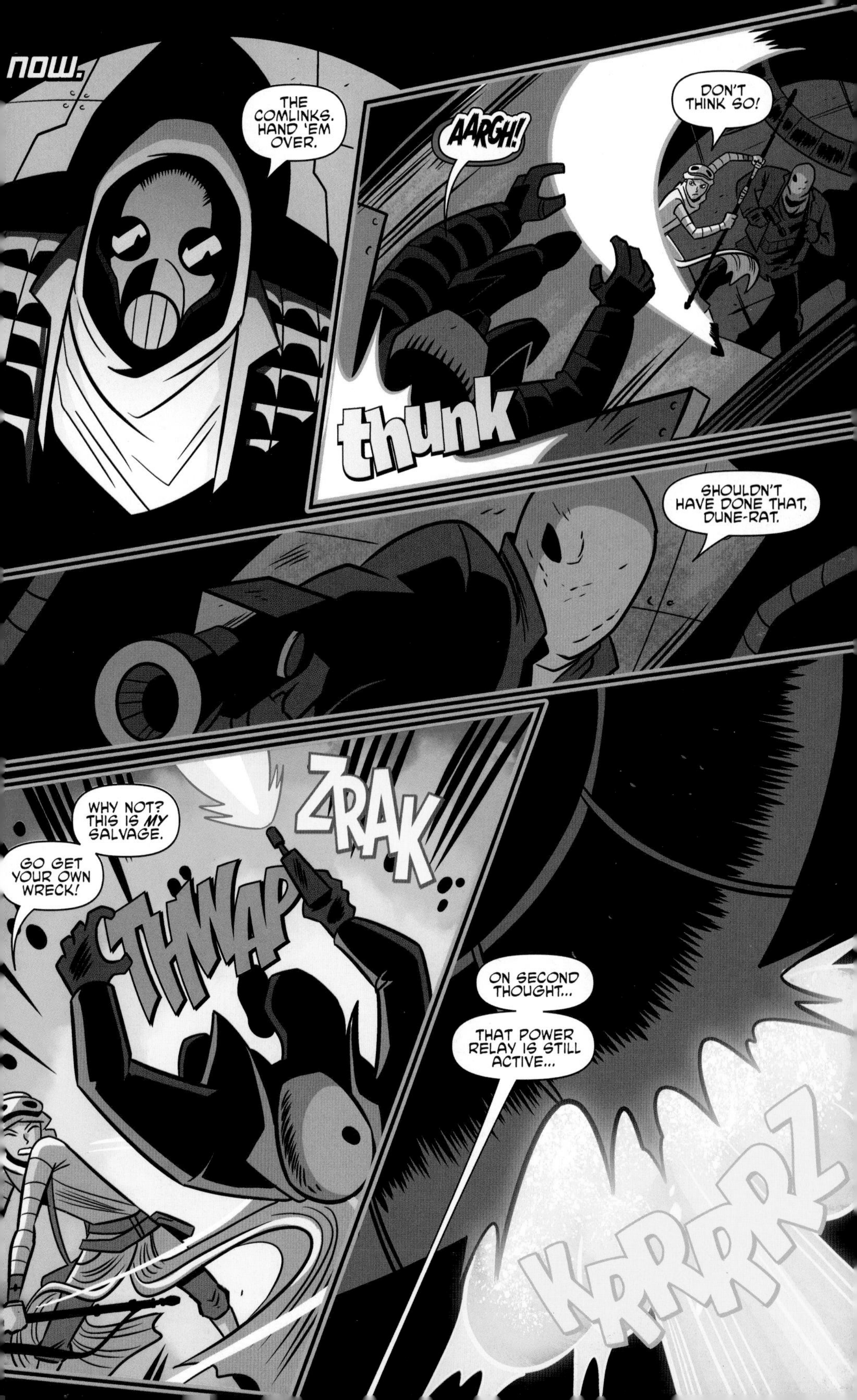
NOW.
THE COMLINKS. HAND 'EM OVER.
AARGH!
DON'T THINK SO!
THUNK
SHOULDN'T HAVE DONE THAT, DUNE-RAT.
WHY NOT? THIS IS MY SALVAGE.
GO GET YOUR OWN WRECK!
ZRAK
THWAP
ON SECOND THOUGHT...
THAT POWER RELAY IS STILL ACTIVE...
KRRRRZ

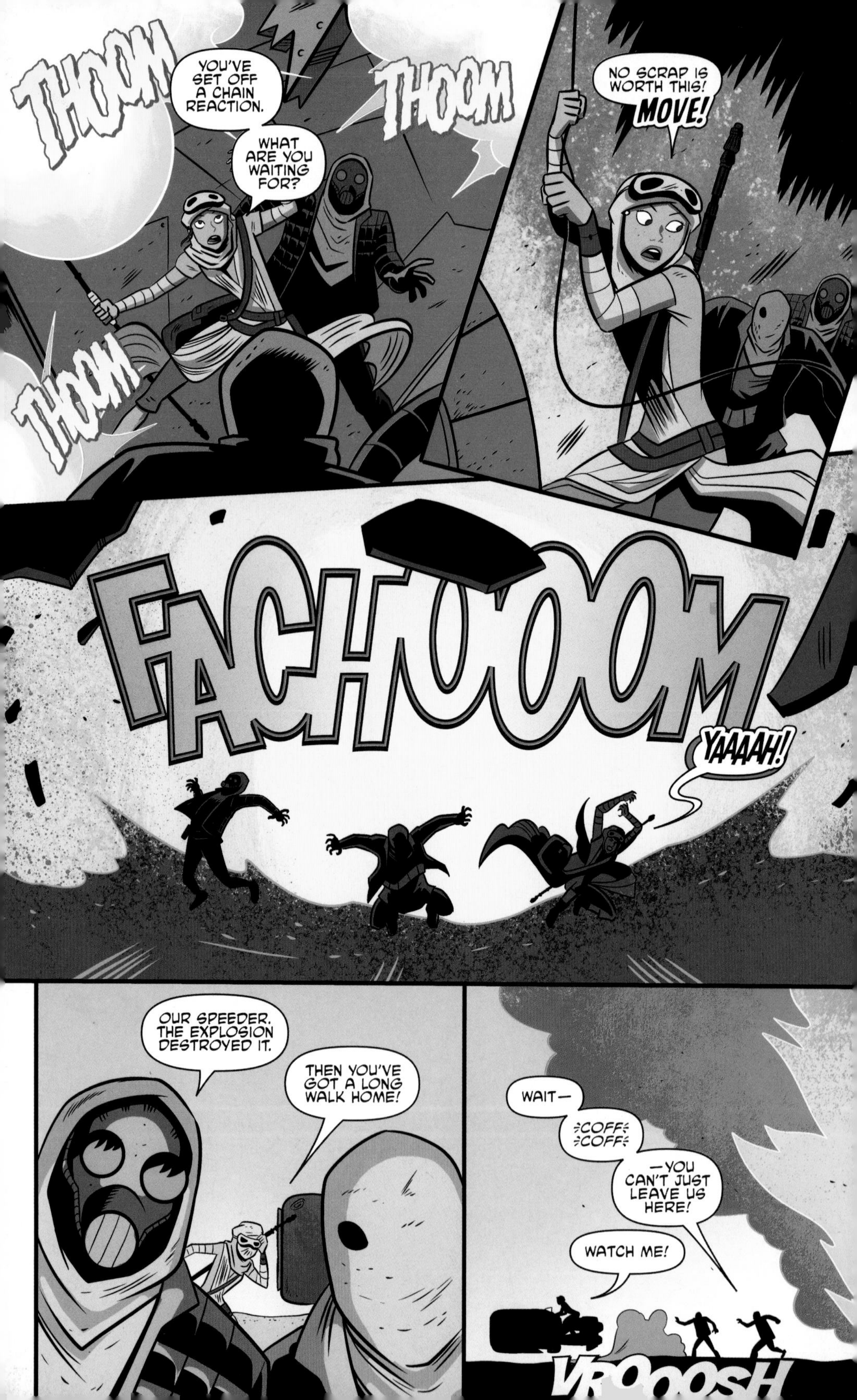
THOOM
YOU'VE SET OFF A CHAIN REACTION.
WHAT ARE YOU WAITING FOR?
THOOM
THOOM
NO SCRAP IS WORTH THIS! MOVE!
FACHOOOM
YAAAAH!
OUR SPEEDER. THE EXPLOSION DESTROYED IT.
THEN YOU'VE GOT A LONG WALK HOME!
WAIT—
COFF COFF
—YOU CAN'T JUST LEAVE US HERE!
WATCH ME!
VROOOOSH

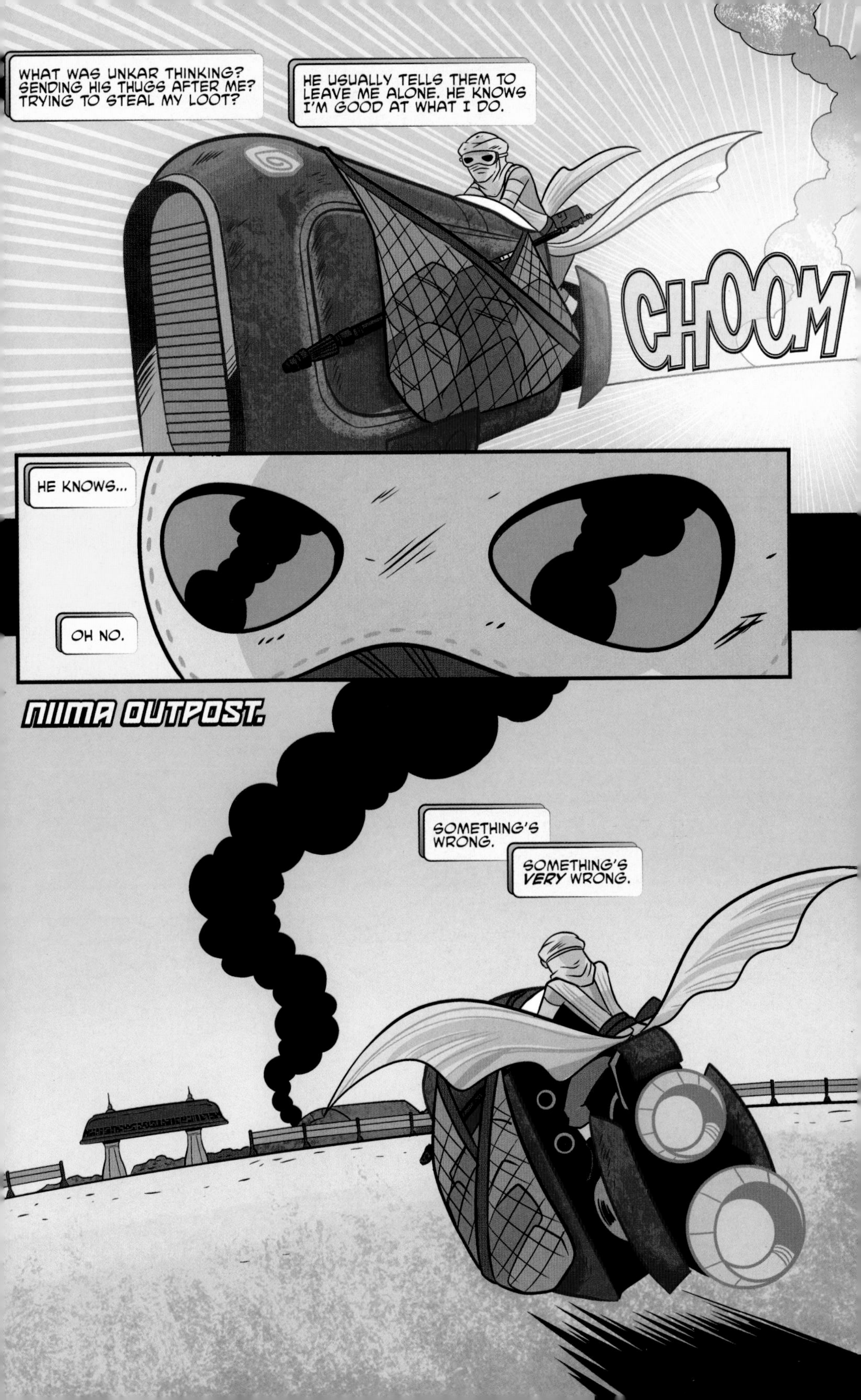
WHAT WAS UNKAR THINKING? SENDING HIS THUGS AFTER ME? TRYING TO STEAL MY LOOT?
HE USUALLY TELLS THEM TO LEAVE ME ALONE. HE KNOWS I'M GOOD AT WHAT I DO.
CHOOM
HE KNOWS...
OH NO.
NIIMA OUTPOST.
SOMETHING'S WRONG.
SOMETHING'S VERY WRONG.

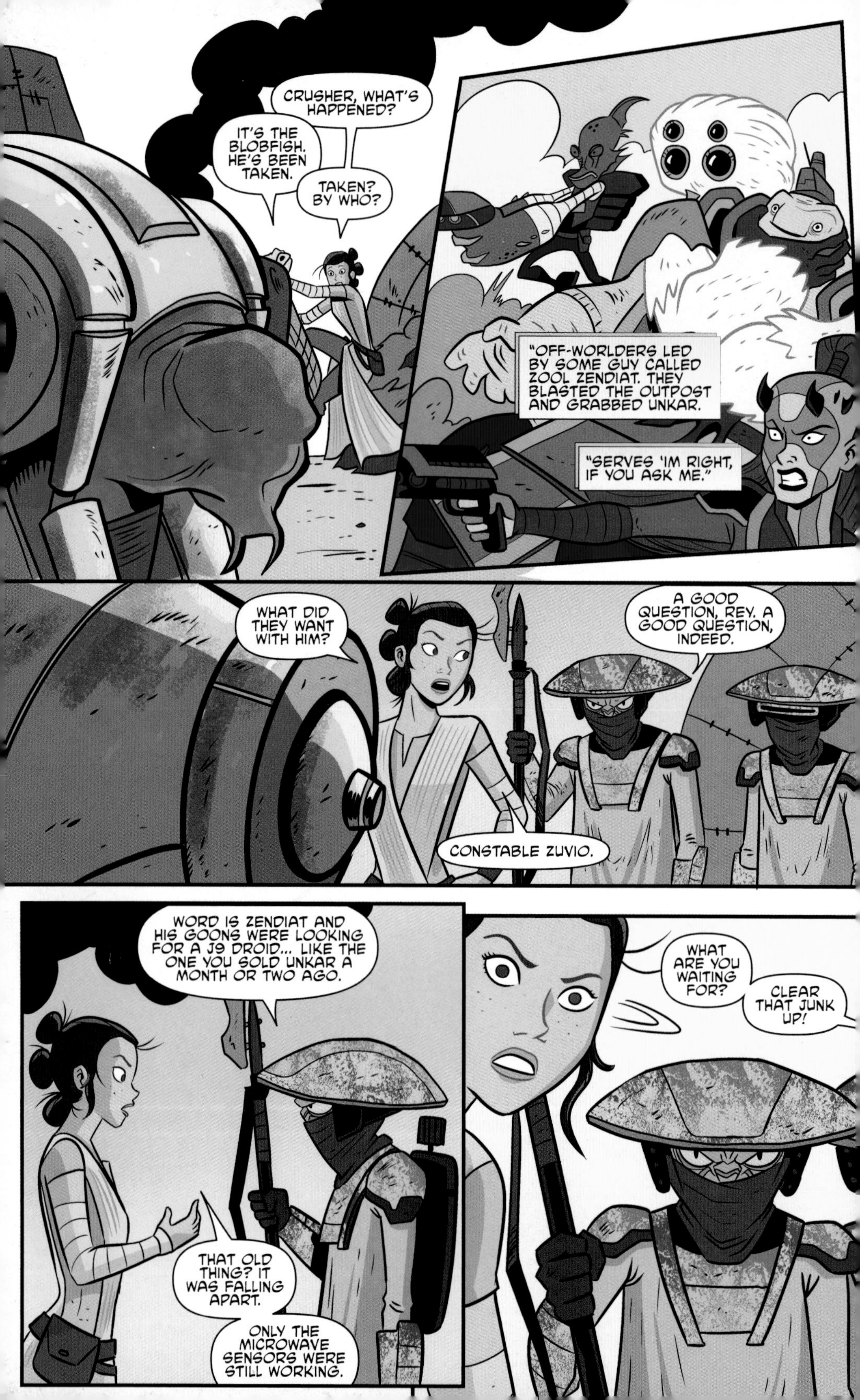
CRUSHER, WHAT'S HAPPENED?
IT'S THE BLOBFISH. HE'S BEEN TAKEN.
TAKEN? BY WHO?
"OFF-WORLDERS LED BY SOME GUY CALLED ZOOL ZENDIAT. THEY BLASTED THE OUTPOST AND GRABBED UNKAR.
"SERVES 'IM RIGHT, IF YOU ASK ME."
WHAT DID THEY WANT WITH HIM?
A GOOD QUESTION, REY. A GOOD QUESTION, INDEED.
CONSTABLE ZUVIO.
WORD IS ZENDIAT AND HIS GOONS WERE LOOKING FOR A J9 DROID... LIKE THE ONE YOU SOLD UNKAR A MONTH OR TWO AGO.
THAT OLD THING? IT WAS FALLING APART.
ONLY THE MICROWAVE SENSORS WERE STILL WORKING.
WHAT ARE YOU WAITING FOR?
CLEAR THAT JUNK UP!

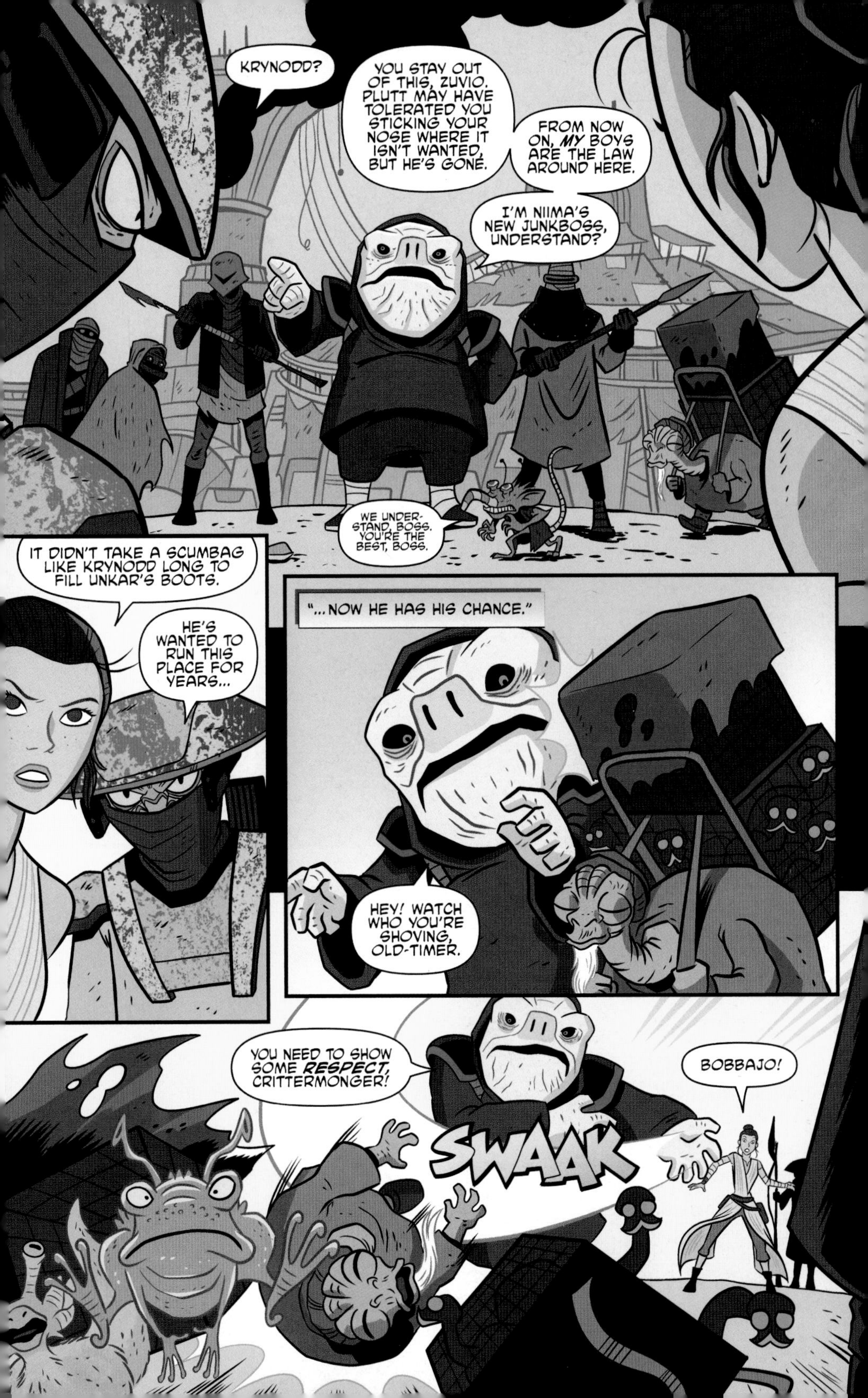
KRYNODD?
YOU STAY OUT OF THIS, ZUVIO. PLUTT MAY HAVE TOLERATED YOU STICKING YOUR NOSE WHERE IT ISN'T WANTED, BUT HE'S GONE.
FROM NOW ON, *MY* BOYS ARE THE LAW AROUND HERE.
I'M NIIMA'S NEW JUNKBOSS, UNDERSTAND?
WE UNDERSTAND, BOSS. YOU'RE THE BEST, BOSS.
IT DIDN'T TAKE A SCUMBAG LIKE KRYNODD LONG TO FILL UNKAR'S BOOTS.
HE'S WANTED TO RUN THIS PLACE FOR YEARS...
"...NOW HE HAS HIS CHANCE."
HEY! WATCH WHO YOU'RE SHOVING, OLD-TIMER.
YOU NEED TO SHOW SOME ***RESPECT***, CRITTERMONGER!
BOBBAJO!
SWAAK

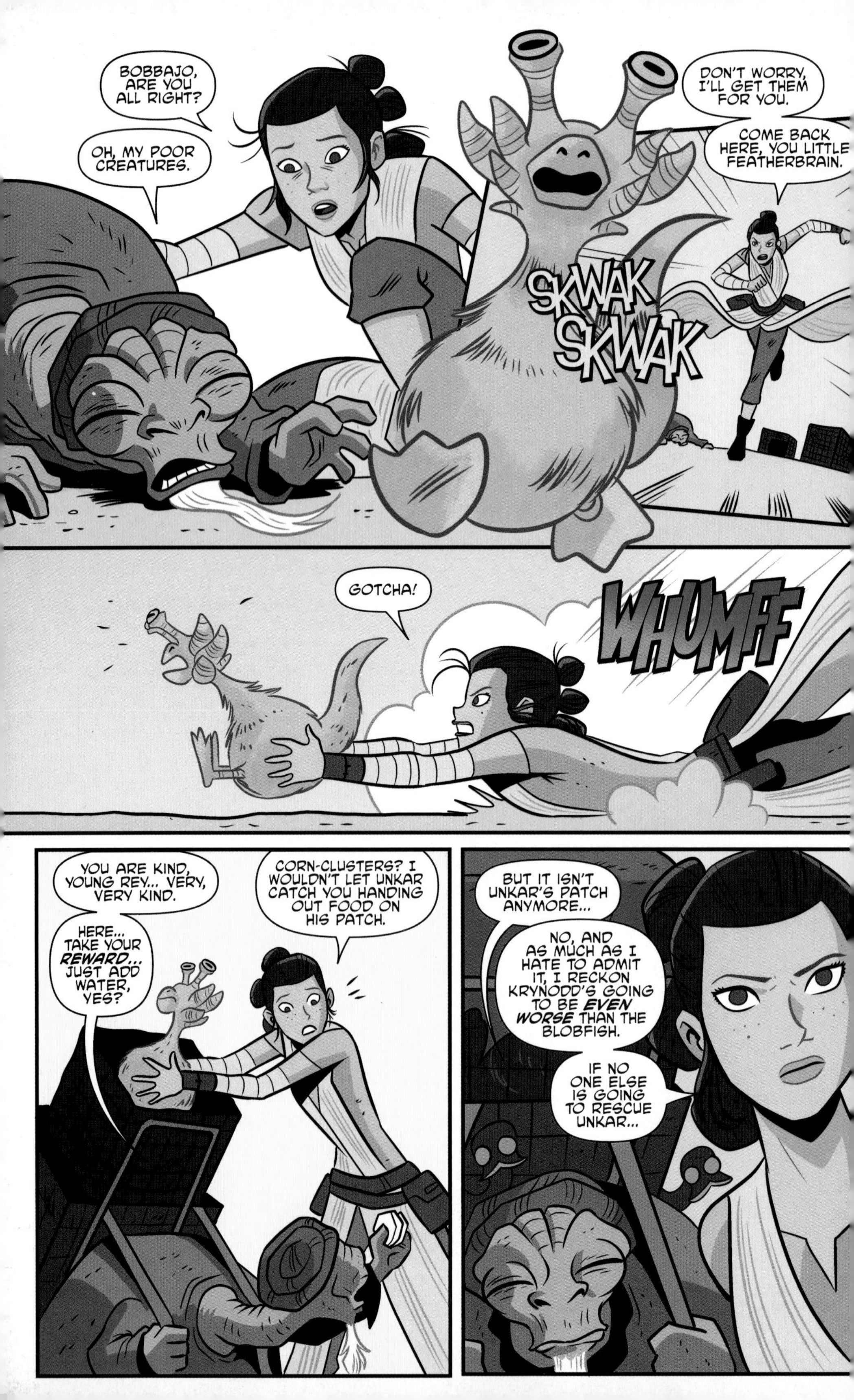
BOBBAJO, ARE YOU ALL RIGHT?
OH, MY POOR CREATURES.
DON'T WORRY, I'LL GET THEM FOR YOU.
COME BACK HERE, YOU LITTLE FEATHERBRAIN.
SKWAK SKWAK
GOTCHA!
WHUMFF
YOU ARE KIND, YOUNG REY... VERY, VERY KIND.
HERE... TAKE YOUR *REWARD*... JUST ADD WATER, YES?
CORN-CLUSTERS? I WOULDN'T LET UNKAR CATCH YOU HANDING OUT FOOD ON HIS PATCH.
BUT IT ISN'T UNKAR'S PATCH ANYMORE...
NO, AND AS MUCH AS I HATE TO ADMIT IT, I RECKON KRYNODD'S GOING TO BE *EVEN WORSE* THAN THE BLOBFISH.
IF NO ONE ELSE IS GOING TO RESCUE UNKAR...

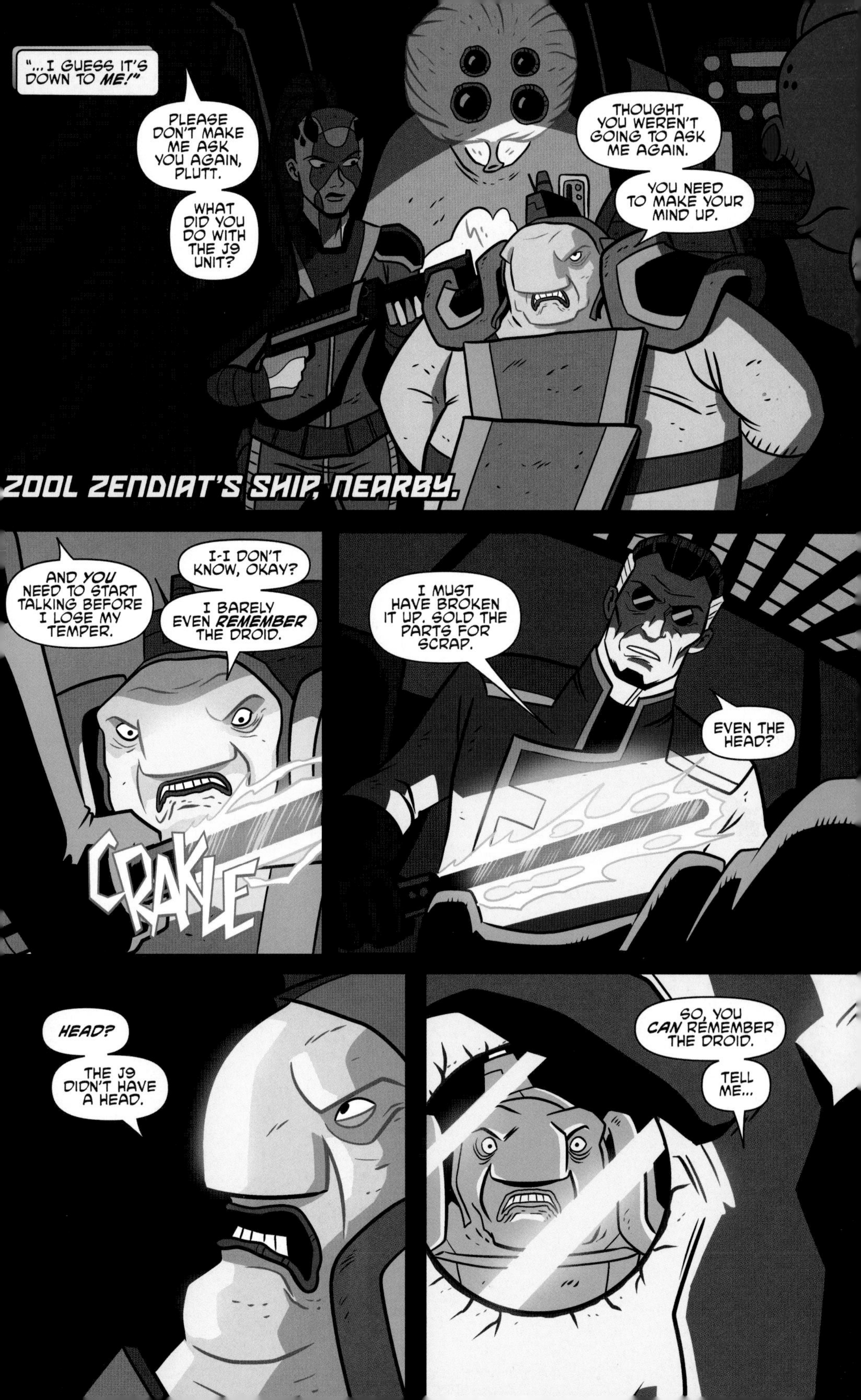
"...I GUESS IT'S DOWN TO *ME!*"
PLEASE DON'T MAKE ME ASK YOU AGAIN, PLUTT.
WHAT DID YOU DO WITH THE J9 UNIT?
THOUGHT YOU WEREN'T GOING TO ASK ME AGAIN.
YOU NEED TO MAKE YOUR MIND UP.
ZOOL ZENDIAT'S SHIP, NEARBY.
AND *YOU* NEED TO START TALKING BEFORE I LOSE MY TEMPER.
I-I DON'T KNOW, OKAY?
I BARELY EVEN ***REMEMBER*** THE DROID.
CRAKLE
I MUST HAVE BROKEN IT UP. SOLD THE PARTS FOR SCRAP.
EVEN THE HEAD?
HEAD?
THE J9 DIDN'T HAVE A HEAD.
SO, YOU *CAN* REMEMBER THE DROID.
TELL ME...

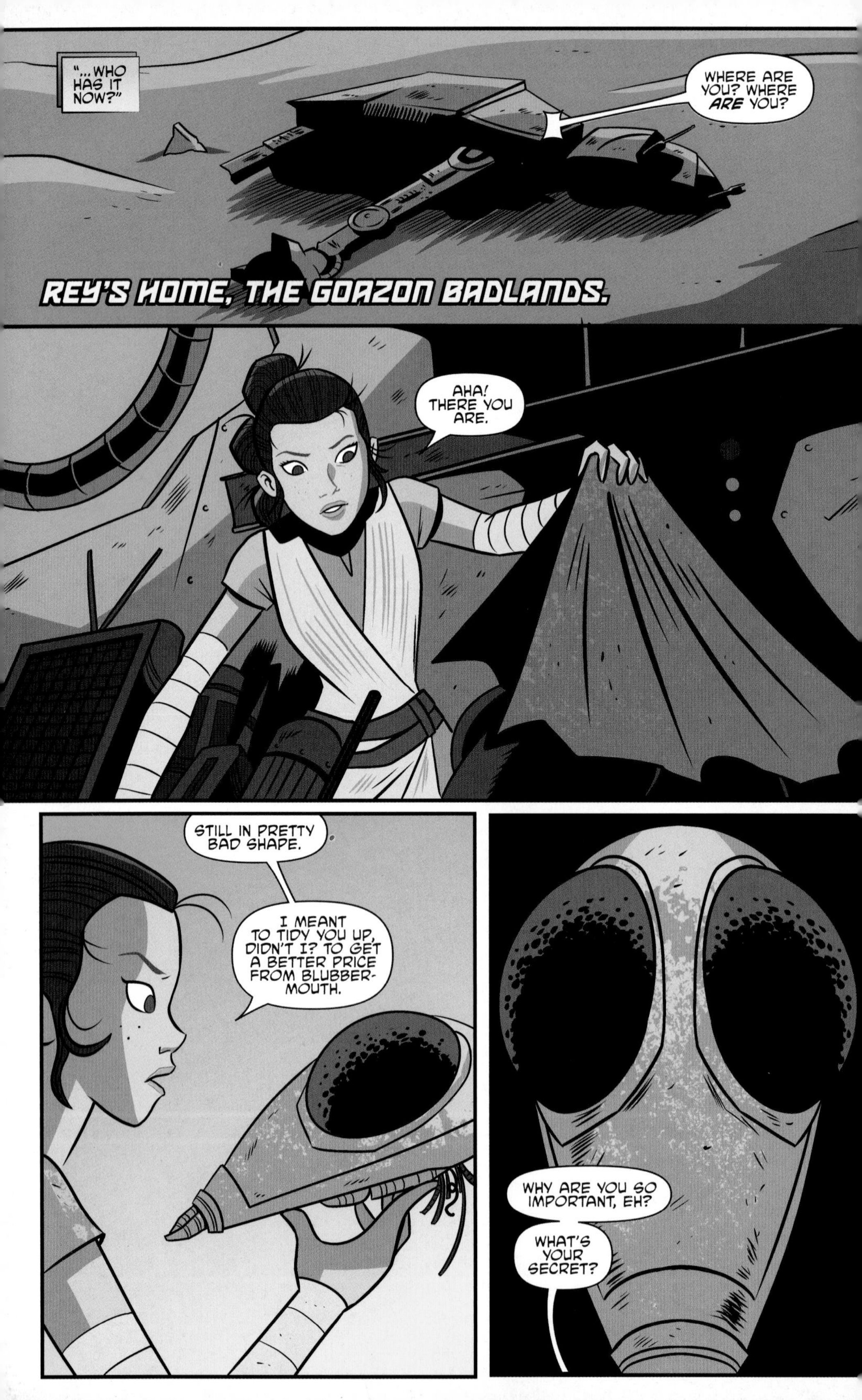
"...WHO HAS IT NOW?"
WHERE ARE YOU? WHERE *ARE* YOU?
REY'S HOME, THE GOAZON BADLANDS.
AHA! THERE YOU ARE.
STILL IN PRETTY BAD SHAPE.
I MEANT TO TIDY YOU UP, DIDN'T I? TO GET A BETTER PRICE FROM BLUBBER-MOUTH.
WHY ARE YOU SO IMPORTANT, EH?
WHAT'S YOUR SECRET?

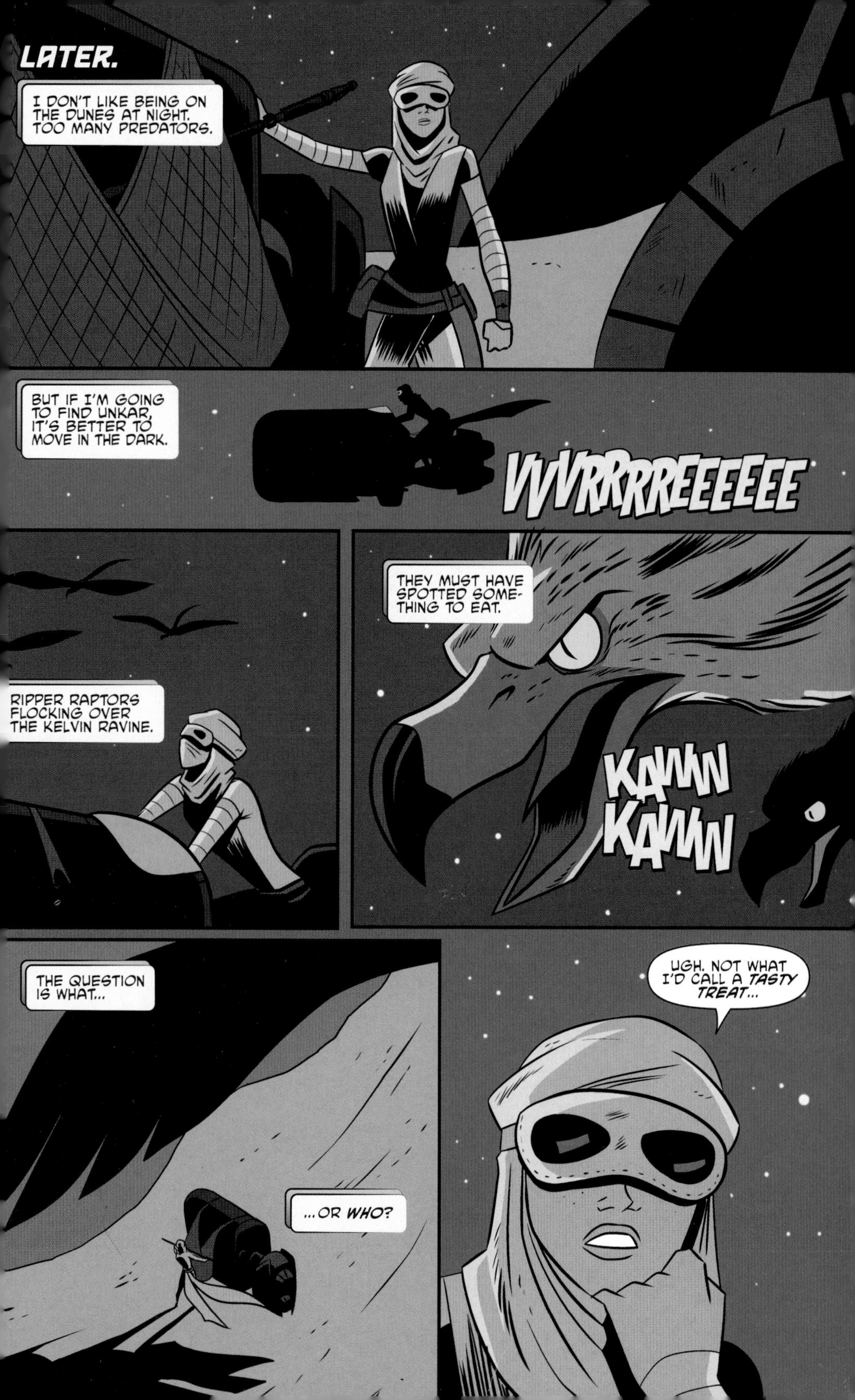
LATER.
I DON'T LIKE BEING ON THE DUNES AT NIGHT. TOO MANY PREDATORS.
BUT IF I'M GOING TO FIND UNKAR, IT'S BETTER TO MOVE IN THE DARK.
VVVRRRRREEEEEE
RIPPER RAPTORS FLOCKING OVER THE KELVIN RAVINE.
THEY MUST HAVE SPOTTED SOME-THING TO EAT.
KAWW KAWW
THE QUESTION IS WHAT...
...OR WHO?
UGH. NOT WHAT I'D CALL A TASTY TREAT...

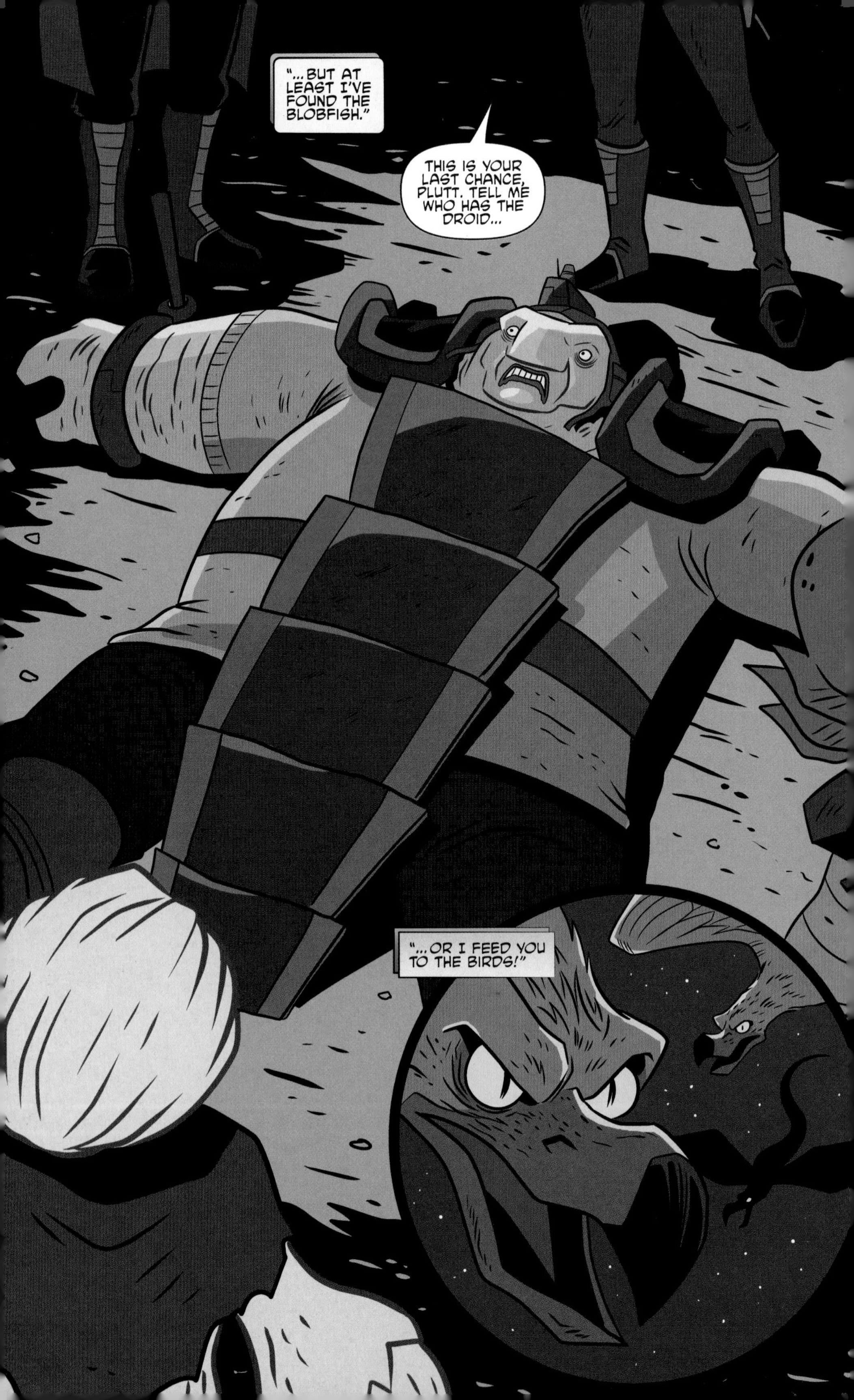
"...BUT AT LEAST I'VE FOUND THE BLOBFISH."
THIS IS YOUR LAST CHANCE, PLUTT. TELL ME WHO HAS THE DROID...
"...OR I FEED YOU TO THE BIRDS!"

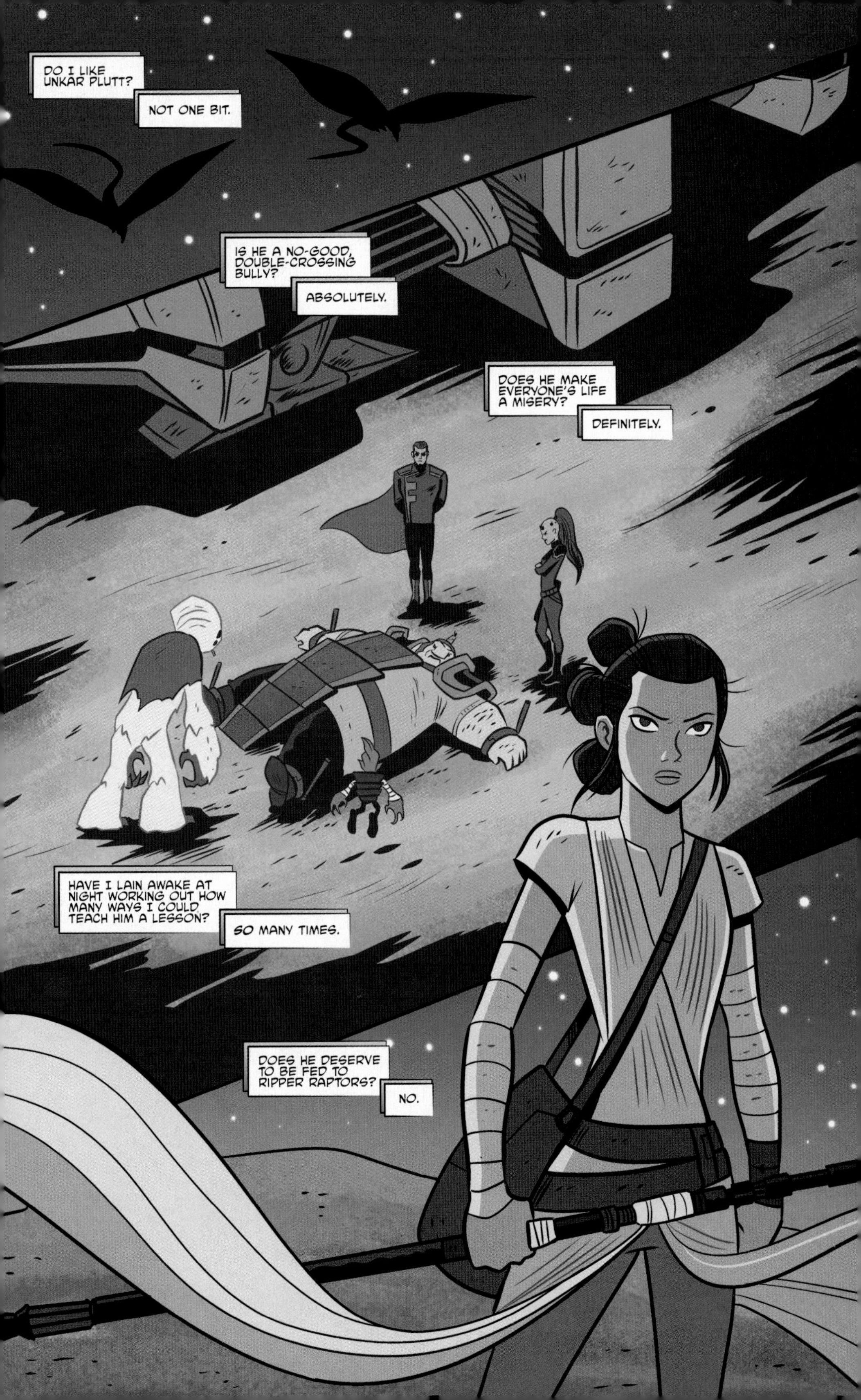
DO I LIKE UNKAR PLUTT?
NOT ONE BIT.
IS HE A NO-GOOD, DOUBLE-CROSSING BULLY?
ABSOLUTELY.
DOES HE MAKE EVERYONE'S LIFE A MISERY?
DEFINITELY.
HAVE I LAIN AWAKE AT NIGHT WORKING OUT HOW MANY WAYS I COULD TEACH HIM A LESSON?
SO MANY TIMES.
DOES HE DESERVE TO BE FED TO RIPPER RAPTORS?
NO.

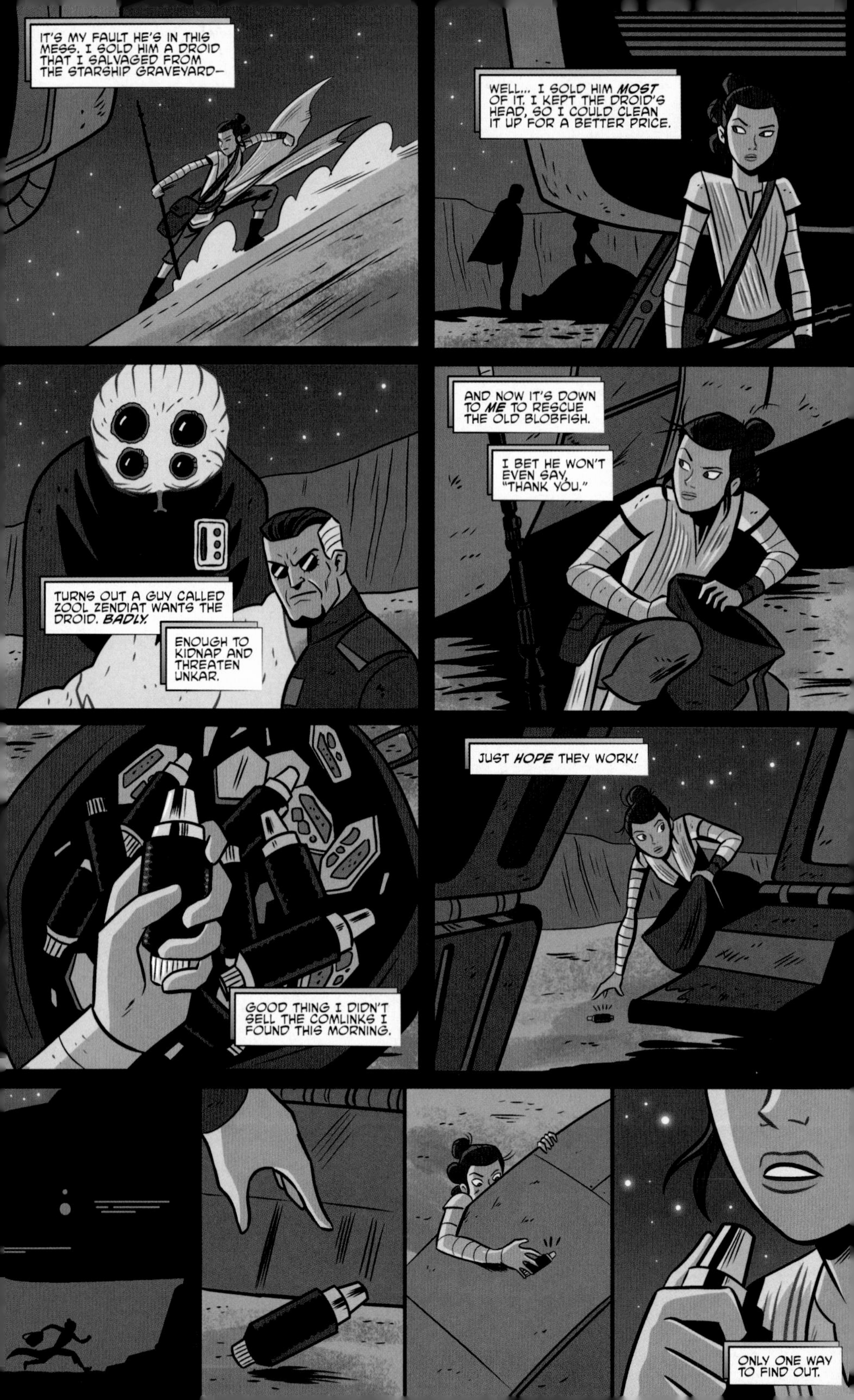
IT'S MY FAULT HE'S IN THIS MESS. I SOLD HIM A DROID THAT I SALVAGED FROM THE STARSHIP GRAVEYARD—
WELL... I SOLD HIM MOST OF IT. I KEPT THE DROID'S HEAD, SO I COULD CLEAN IT UP FOR A BETTER PRICE.
TURNS OUT A GUY CALLED ZOOL ZENDIAT WANTS THE DROID. BADLY.
ENOUGH TO KIDNAP AND THREATEN UNKAR.
AND NOW IT'S DOWN TO ME TO RESCUE THE OLD BLOBFISH.
I BET HE WON'T EVEN SAY, "THANK YOU."
GOOD THING I DIDN'T SELL THE COMLINKS I FOUND THIS MORNING.
JUST HOPE THEY WORK!
ONLY ONE WAY TO FIND OUT.

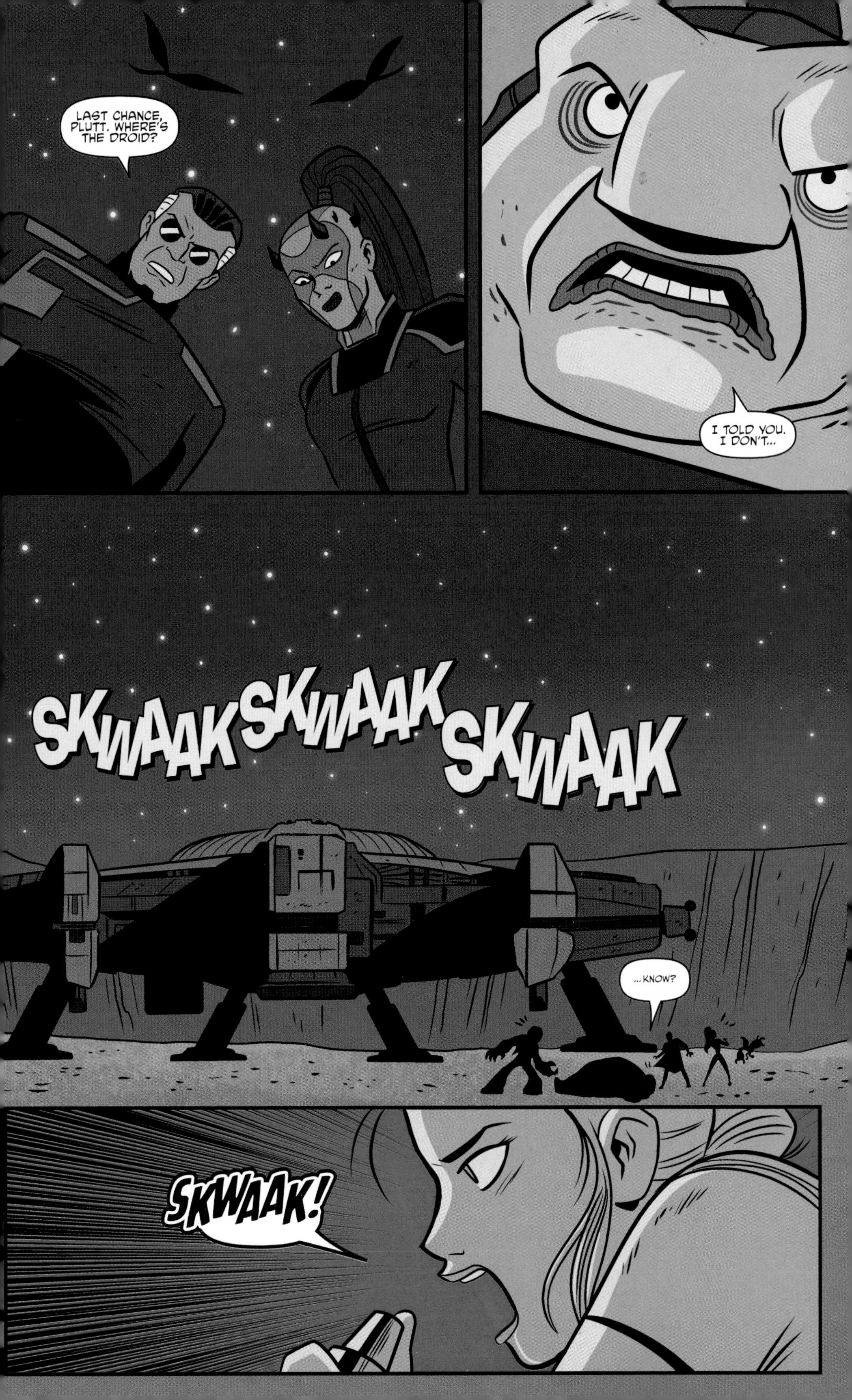
LAST CHANCE, PLUTT. WHERE'S THE DROID?
I TOLD YOU. I DON'T...
SKWAAK SKWAAK SKWAAK
...KNOW?
SKWAAK!

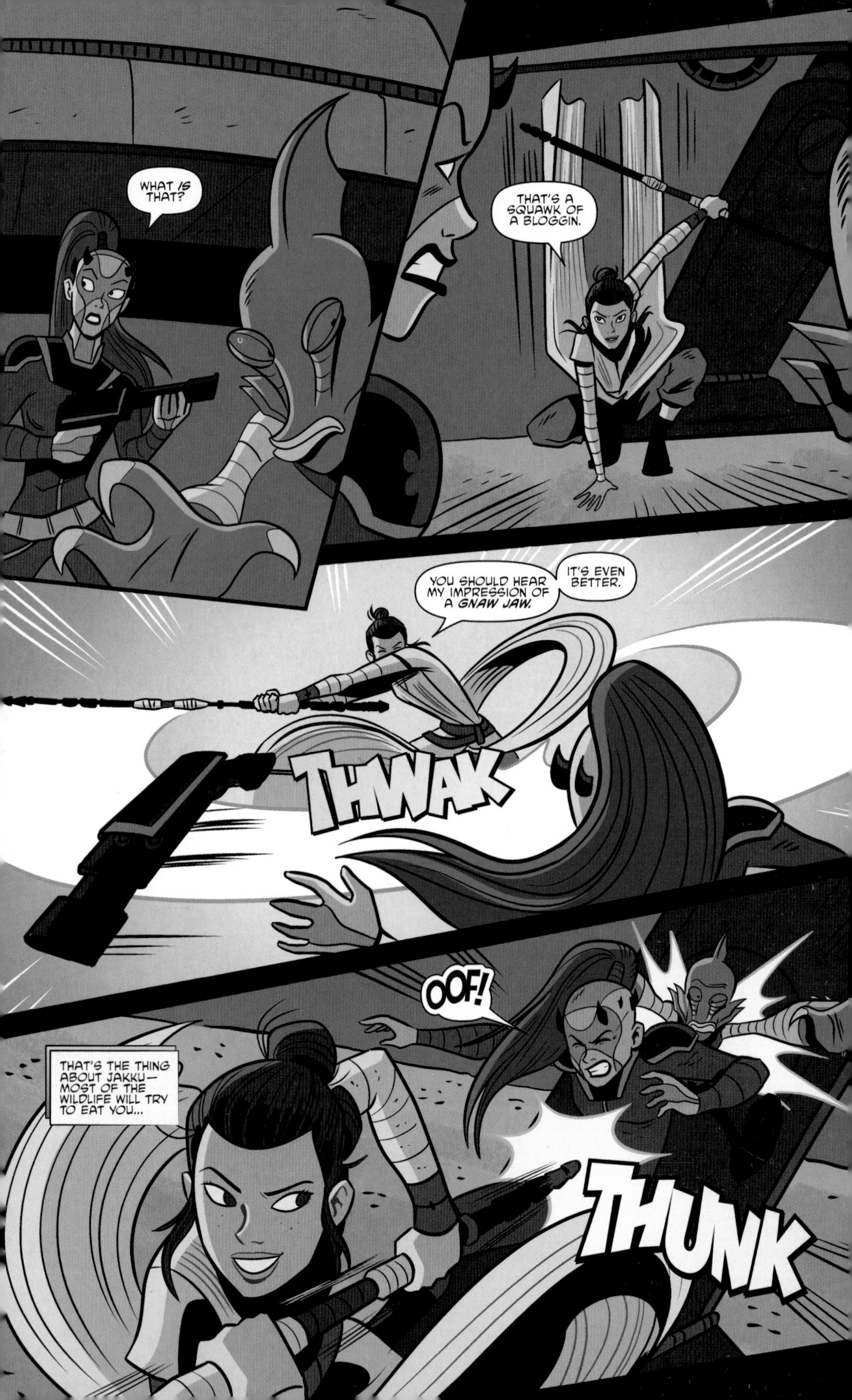
WHAT IS THAT?
THAT'S A SQUAWK OF A BLOGGIN.
YOU SHOULD HEAR MY IMPRESSION OF A GNAW JAW.
IT'S EVEN BETTER.
THWAK
OOF!
THAT'S THE THING ABOUT JAKKU— MOST OF THE WILDLIFE WILL TRY TO EAT YOU...
THUNK

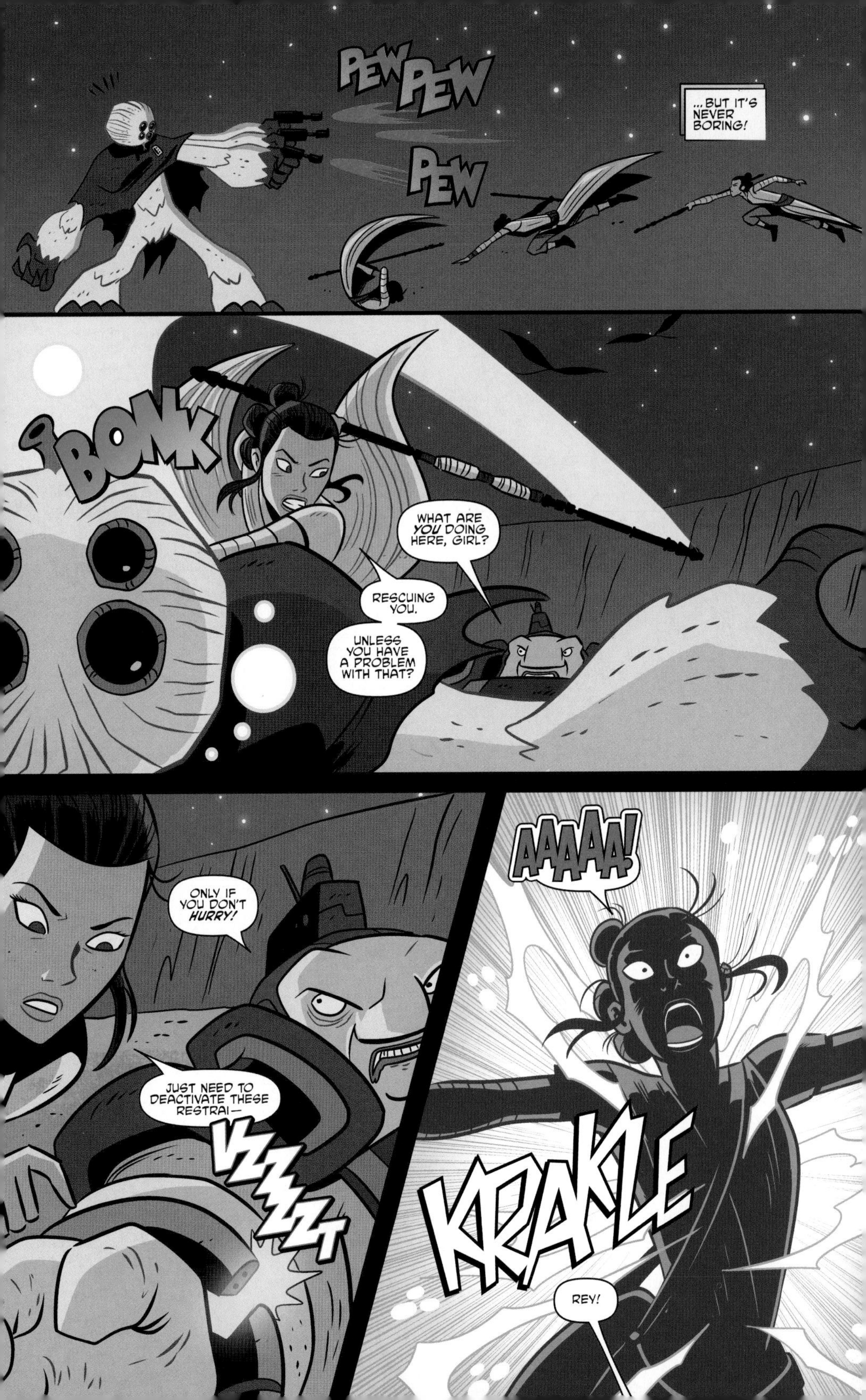
PEW PEW
...BUT IT'S NEVER BORING!
PEW
BONK
WHAT ARE YOU DOING HERE, GIRL?
RESCUING YOU.
UNLESS YOU HAVE A PROBLEM WITH THAT?
ONLY IF YOU DON'T HURRY!
JUST NEED TO DEACTIVATE THESE RESTRAI—
VZZZZT
AAAAA!
KRAKLE
REY!

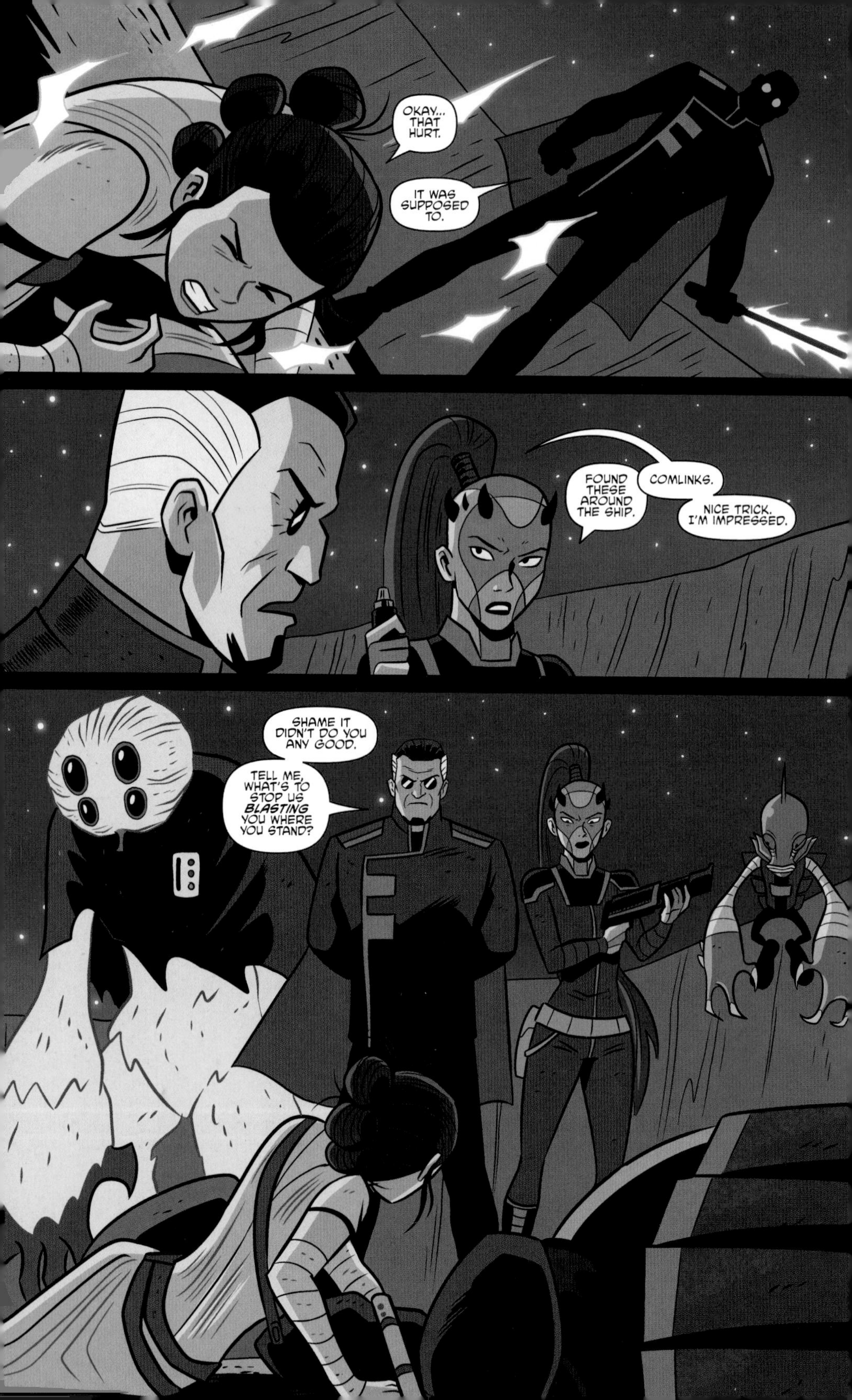
OKAY... THAT HURT.
IT WAS SUPPOSED TO.
FOUND THESE AROUND THE SHIP.
COMLINKS.
NICE TRICK. I'M IMPRESSED.
SHAME IT DIDN'T DO YOU ANY GOOD.
TELL ME, WHAT'S TO STOP US *BLASTING* YOU WHERE YOU STAND?

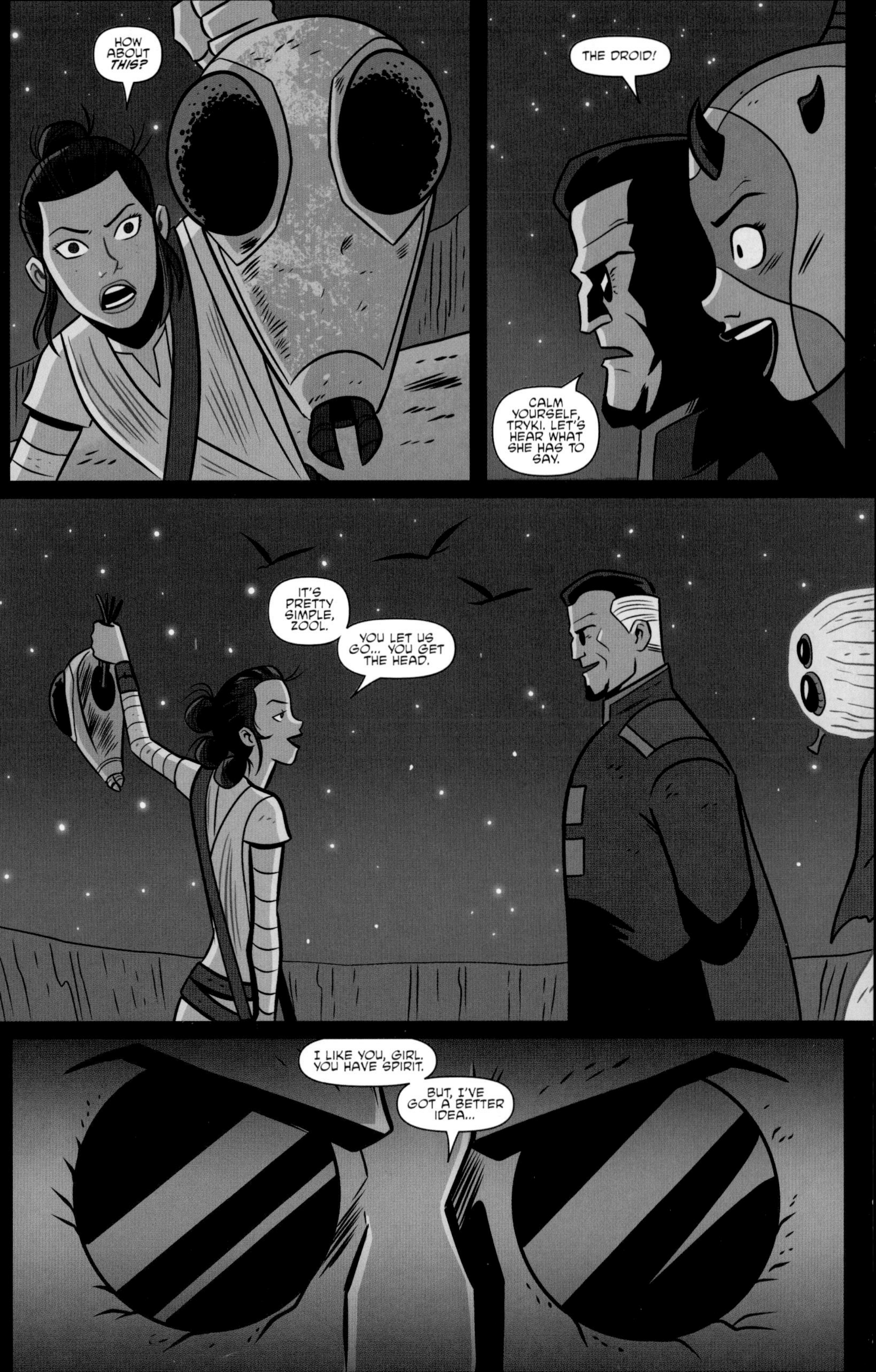
HOW ABOUT THIS?
THE DROID!
CALM YOURSELF, TRYKI. LET'S HEAR WHAT SHE HAS TO SAY.
IT'S PRETTY SIMPLE, ZOOL.
YOU LET US GO... YOU GET THE HEAD.
I LIKE YOU, GIRL. YOU HAVE SPIRIT.
BUT, I'VE GOT A BETTER IDEA...

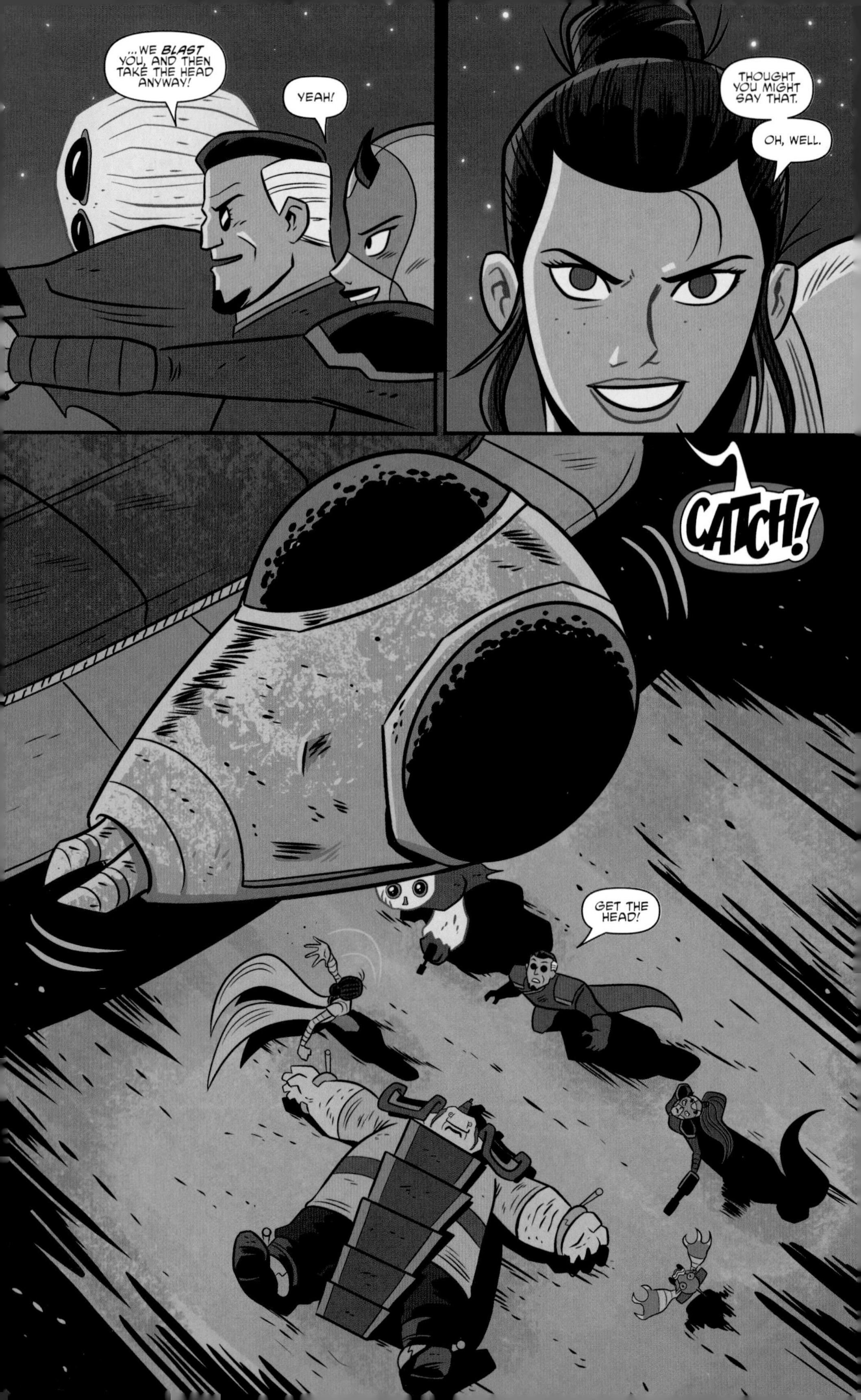
...WE BLAST YOU, AND THEN TAKE THE HEAD ANYWAY!
YEAH!
THOUGHT YOU MIGHT SAY THAT.
OH, WELL.
CATCH!
GET THE HEAD!

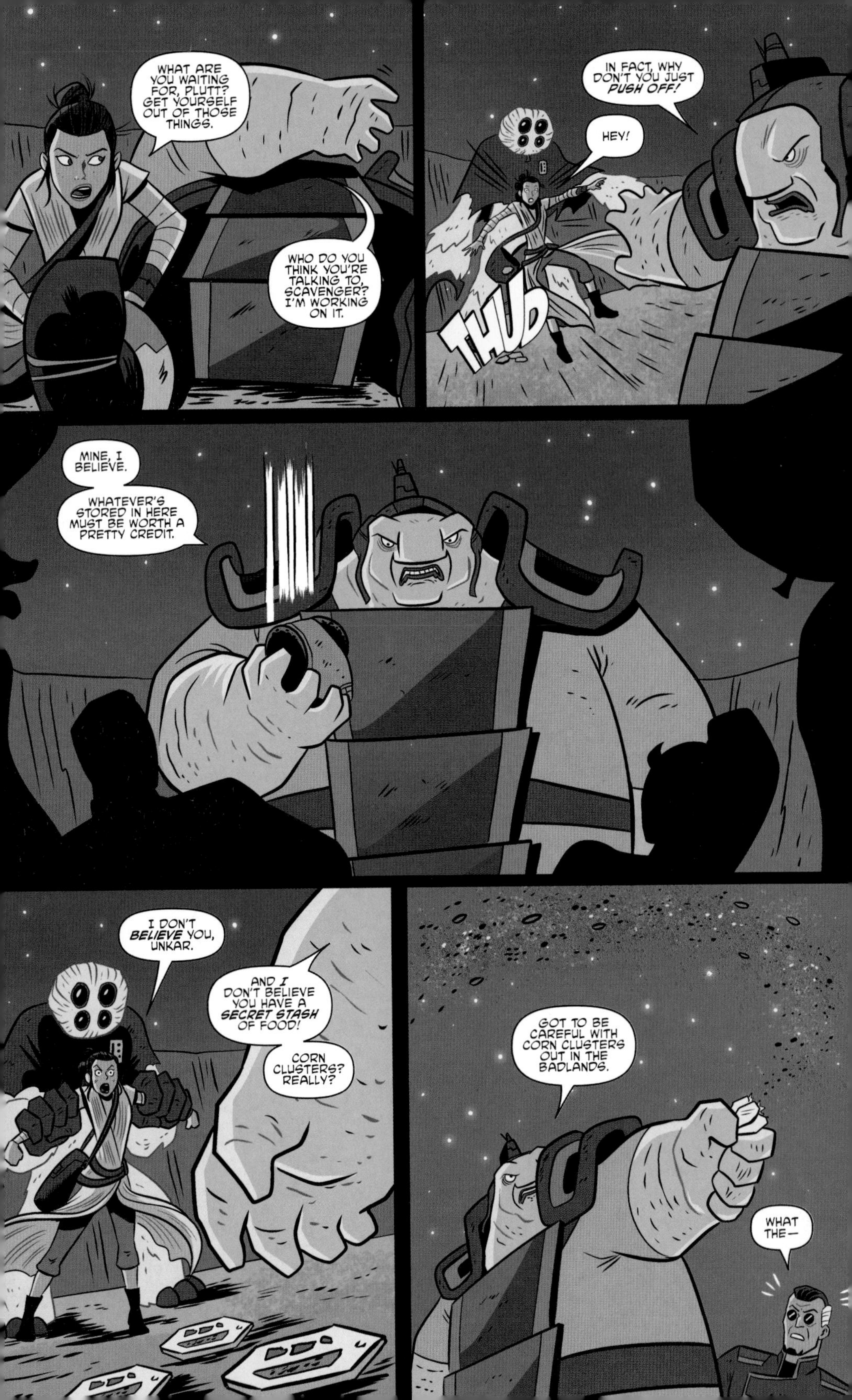
WHAT ARE YOU WAITING FOR, PLUTT? GET YOURSELF OUT OF THOSE THINGS.
WHO DO YOU THINK YOU'RE TALKING TO, SCAVENGER? I'M WORKING ON IT.
IN FACT, WHY DON'T YOU JUST PUSH OFF!
HEY!
THUD
MINE, I BELIEVE.
WHATEVER'S STORED IN HERE MUST BE WORTH A PRETTY CREDIT.
I DON'T BELIEVE YOU, UNKAR.
AND I DON'T BELIEVE YOU HAVE A SECRET STASH OF FOOD!
CORN CLUSTERS? REALLY?
GOT TO BE CAREFUL WITH CORN CLUSTERS OUT IN THE BADLANDS.
WHAT THE—

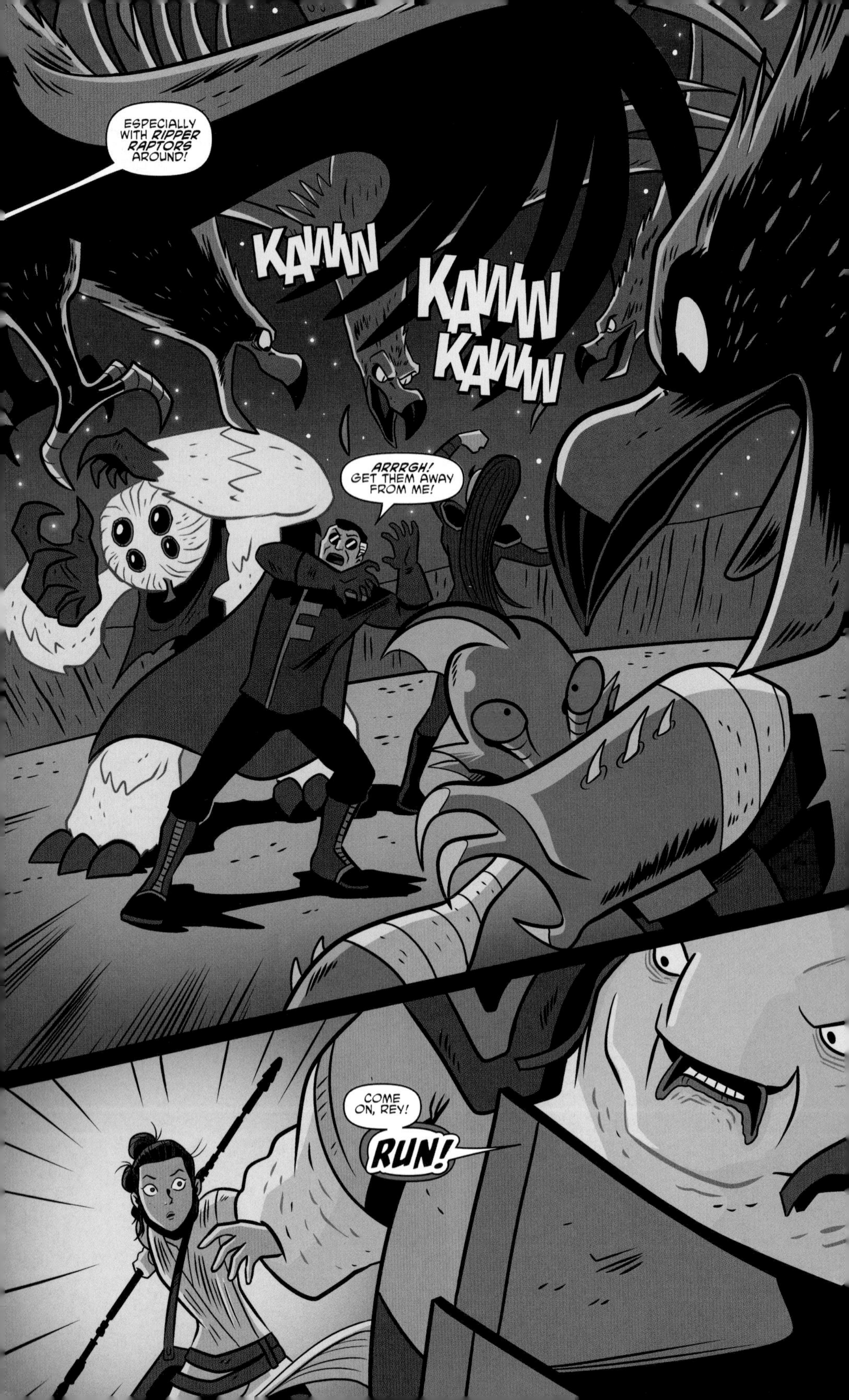
ESPECIALLY WITH RIPPER RAPTORS AROUND!
KAWW
KAWW KAWW
ARRRGH! GET THEM AWAY FROM ME!
COME ON, REY!
RUN!

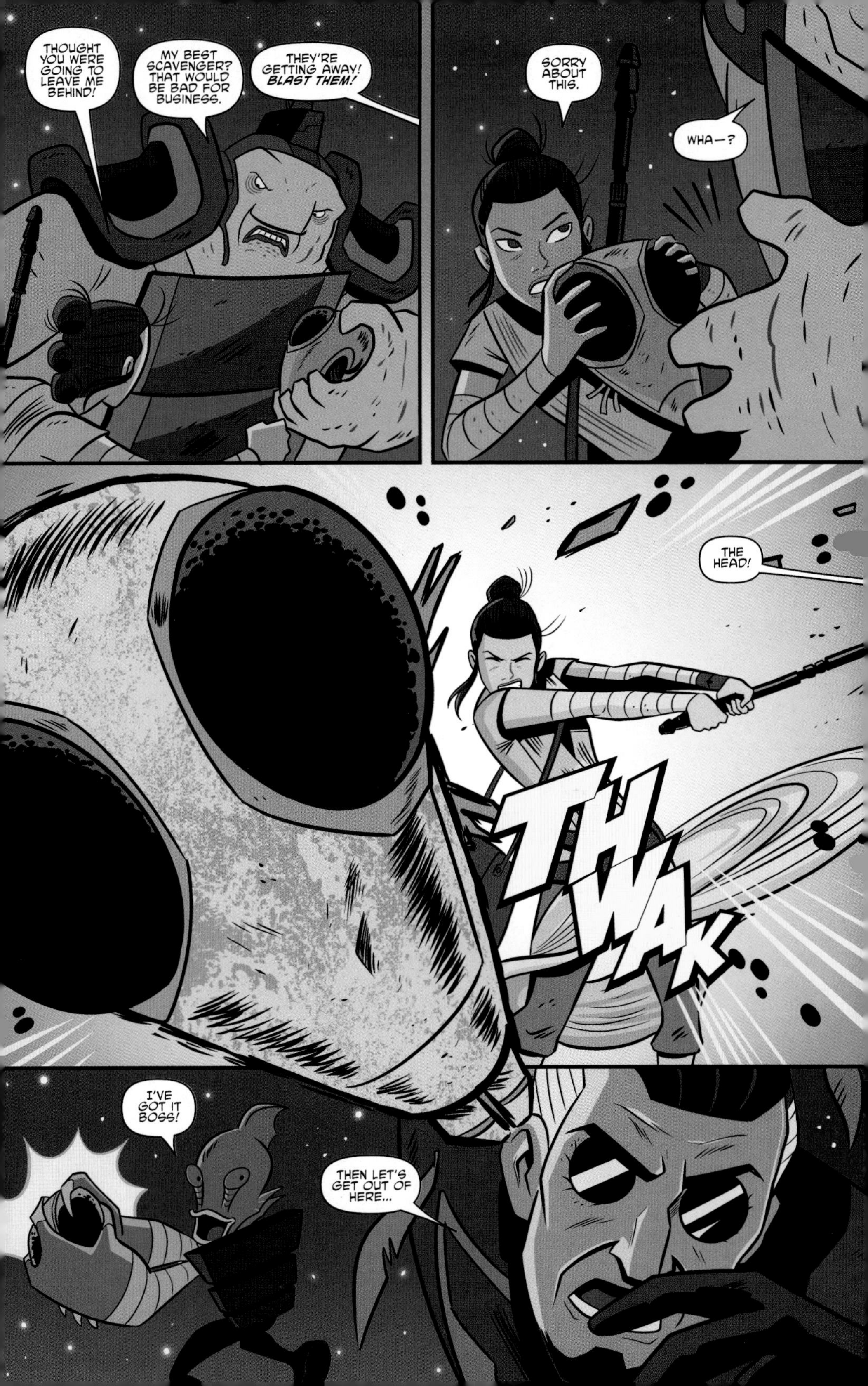
THOUGHT YOU WERE GOING TO LEAVE ME BEHIND!
MY BEST SCAVENGER? THAT WOULD BE BAD FOR BUSINESS.
THEY'RE GETTING AWAY! *BLAST THEM!*
SORRY ABOUT THIS.
WHA—?
THE HEAD!
THWAK
I'VE GOT IT BOSS!
THEN LET'S GET OUT OF HERE...

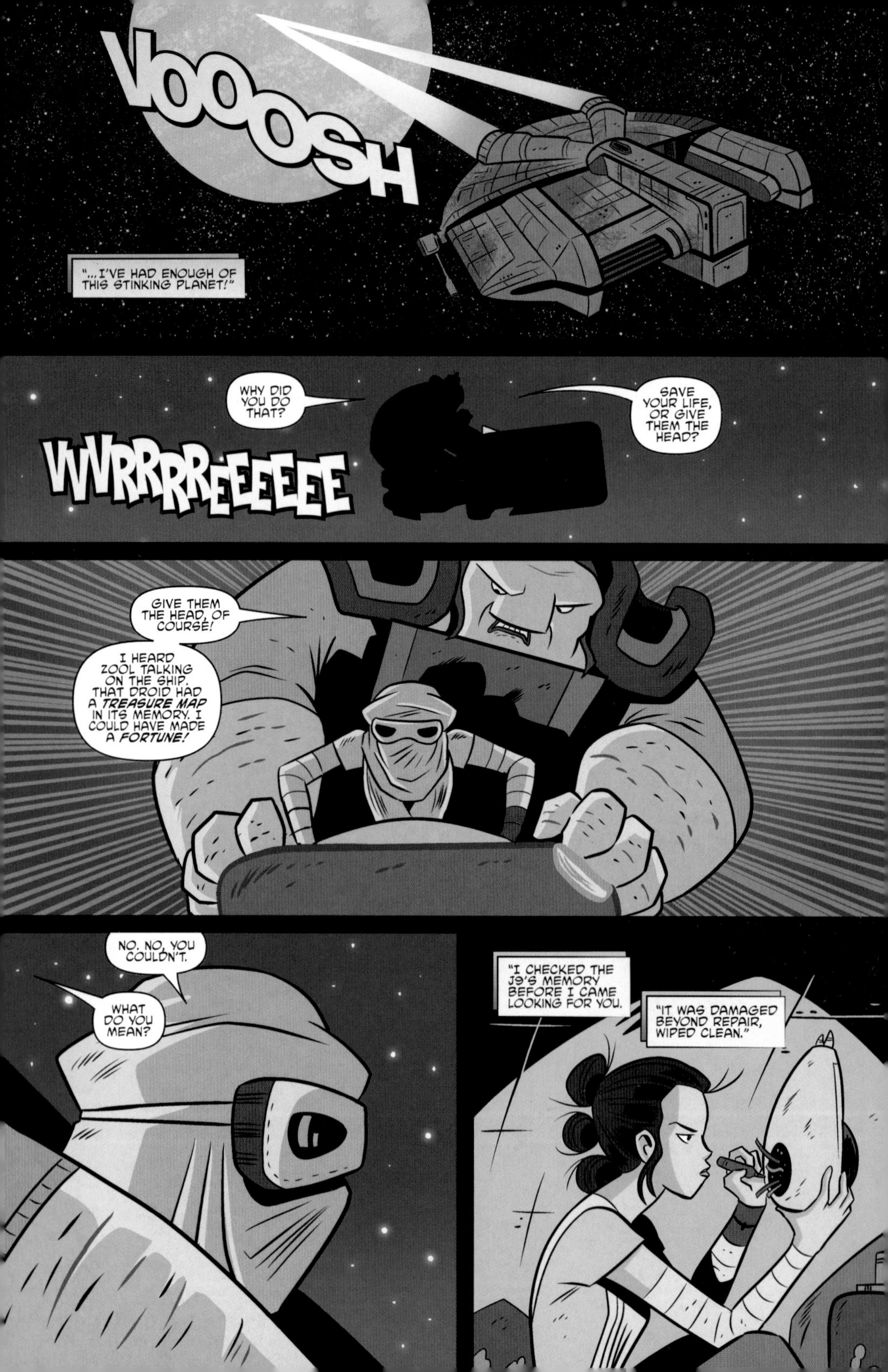
VOOOSH
"...I'VE HAD ENOUGH OF THIS STINKING PLANET!"
WHY DID YOU DO THAT?
SAVE YOUR LIFE, OR GIVE THEM THE HEAD?
VVVRRRREEEEEE
GIVE THEM THE HEAD, OF COURSE!
I HEARD ZOOL TALKING ON THE SHIP. THAT DROID HAD A *TREASURE MAP* IN ITS MEMORY. I COULD HAVE MADE A *FORTUNE!*
NO. NO, YOU COULDN'T.
WHAT DO YOU MEAN?
"I CHECKED THE J9'S MEMORY BEFORE I CAME LOOKING FOR YOU.
"IT WAS DAMAGED BEYOND REPAIR, WIPED CLEAN."

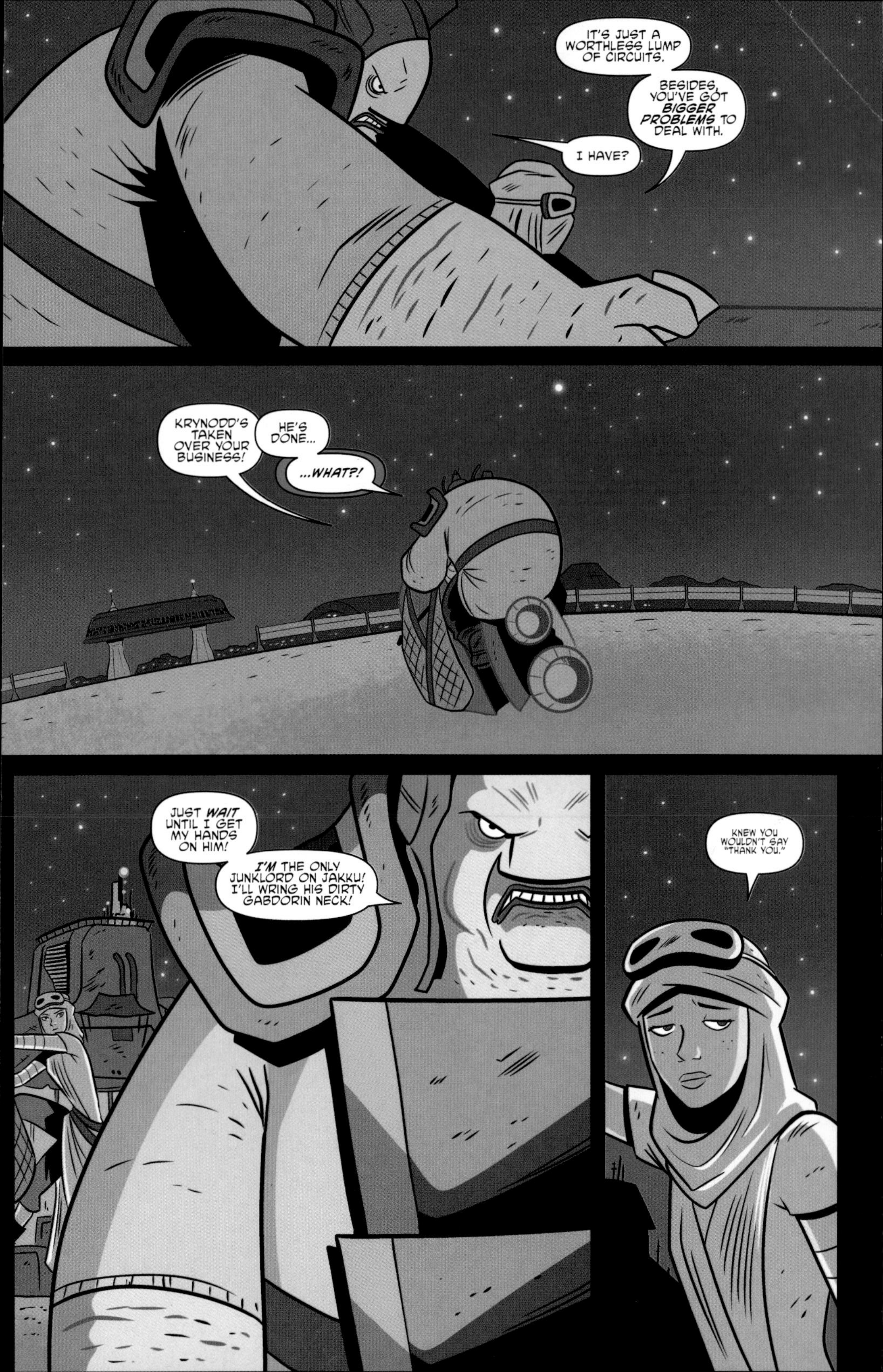
IT'S JUST A WORTHLESS LUMP OF CIRCUITS.
BESIDES, YOU'VE GOT *BIGGER PROBLEMS* TO DEAL WITH.
I HAVE?
KRYNODD'S TAKEN OVER YOUR BUSINESS!
HE'S DONE...
...*WHAT?!*
JUST *WAIT* UNTIL I GET MY HANDS ON HIM!
I'M THE ONLY JUNKLORD ON JAKKU! I'LL WRING HIS DIRTY GABDORIN NECK!
KNEW YOU WOULDN'T SAY "THANK YOU."

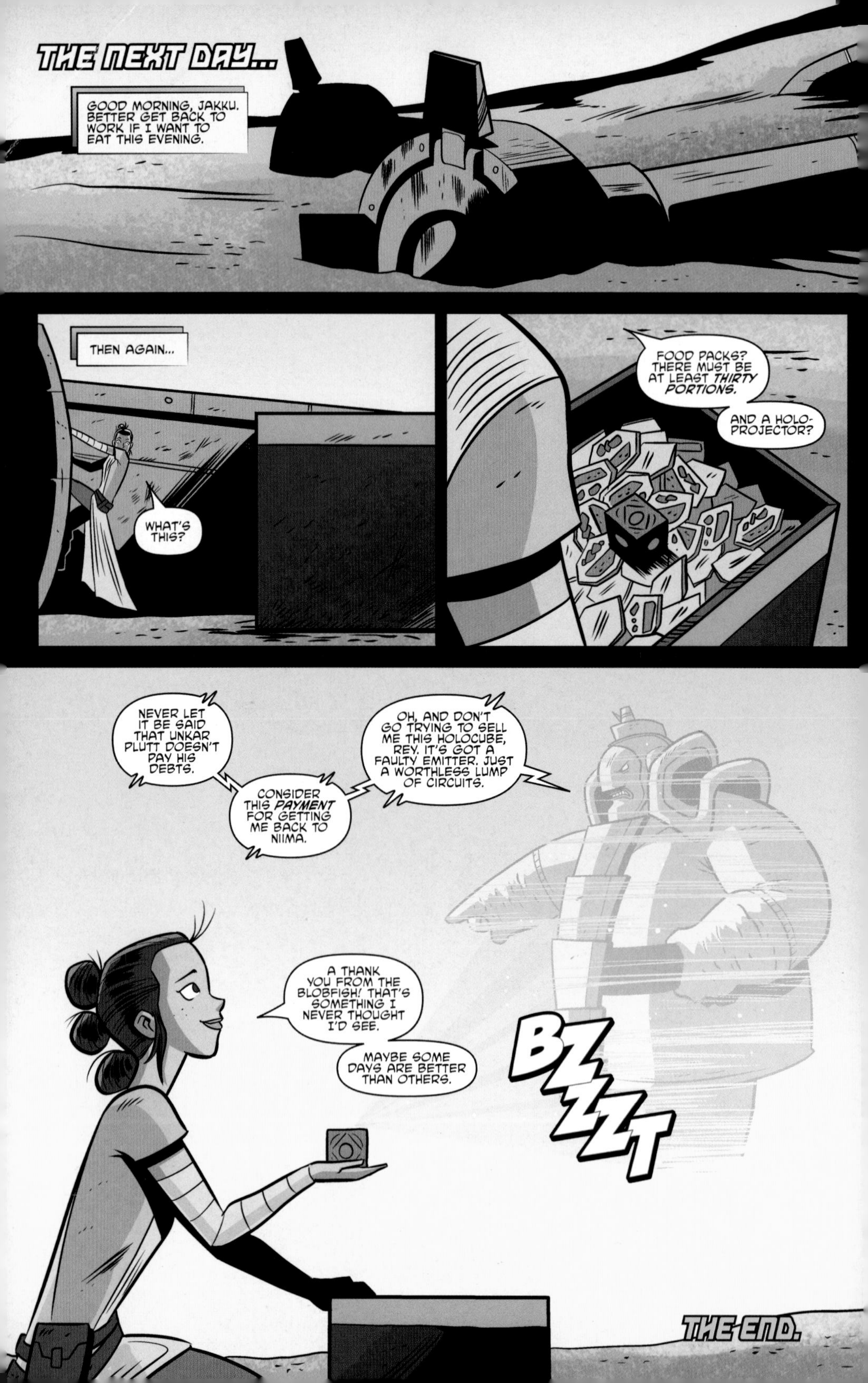
THE NEXT DAY...
GOOD MORNING, JAKKU. BETTER GET BACK TO WORK IF I WANT TO EAT THIS EVENING.
THEN AGAIN...
WHAT'S THIS?
FOOD PACKS? THERE MUST BE AT LEAST THIRTY PORTIONS.
AND A HOLO-PROJECTOR?
NEVER LET IT BE SAID THAT UNKAR PLUTT DOESN'T PAY HIS DEBTS.
CONSIDER THIS PAYMENT FOR GETTING ME BACK TO NIIMA.
OH, AND DON'T GO TRYING TO SELL ME THIS HOLOCUBE, REY. IT'S GOT A FAULTY EMITTER. JUST A WORTHLESS LUMP OF CIRCUITS.
A THANK YOU FROM THE BLOBFISH! THAT'S SOMETHING I NEVER THOUGHT I'D SEE.
MAYBE SOME DAYS ARE BETTER THAN OTHERS.
BZZZT
THE END.

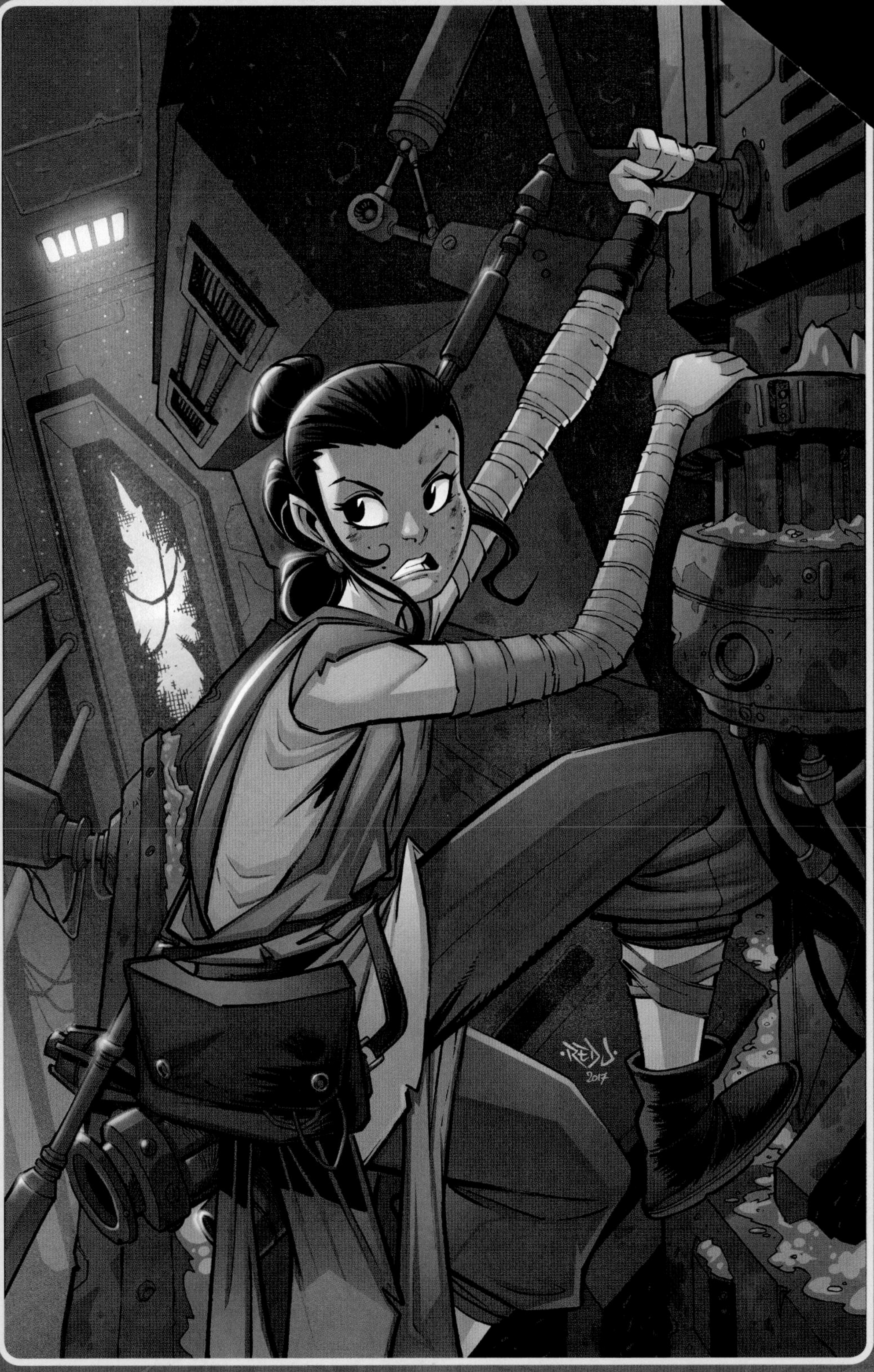

Art by Jon Sommariva

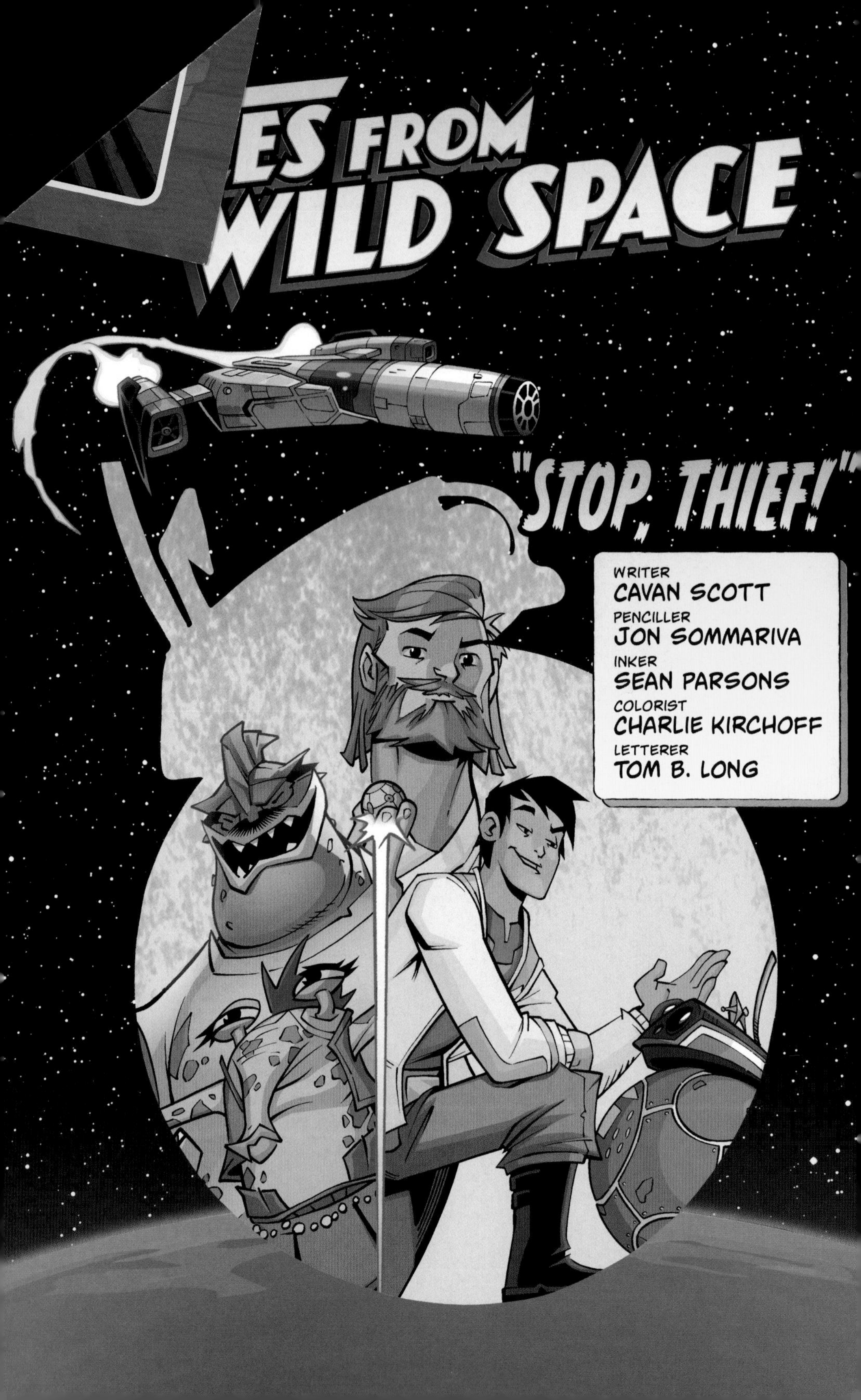
ES FROM
WILD SPACE
"STOP, THIEF!"
WRITER
CAVAN SCOTT
PENCILLER
JON SOMMARIVA
INKER
SEAN PARSONS
COLORIST
CHARLIE KIRCHOFF
LETTERER
TOM B. LONG

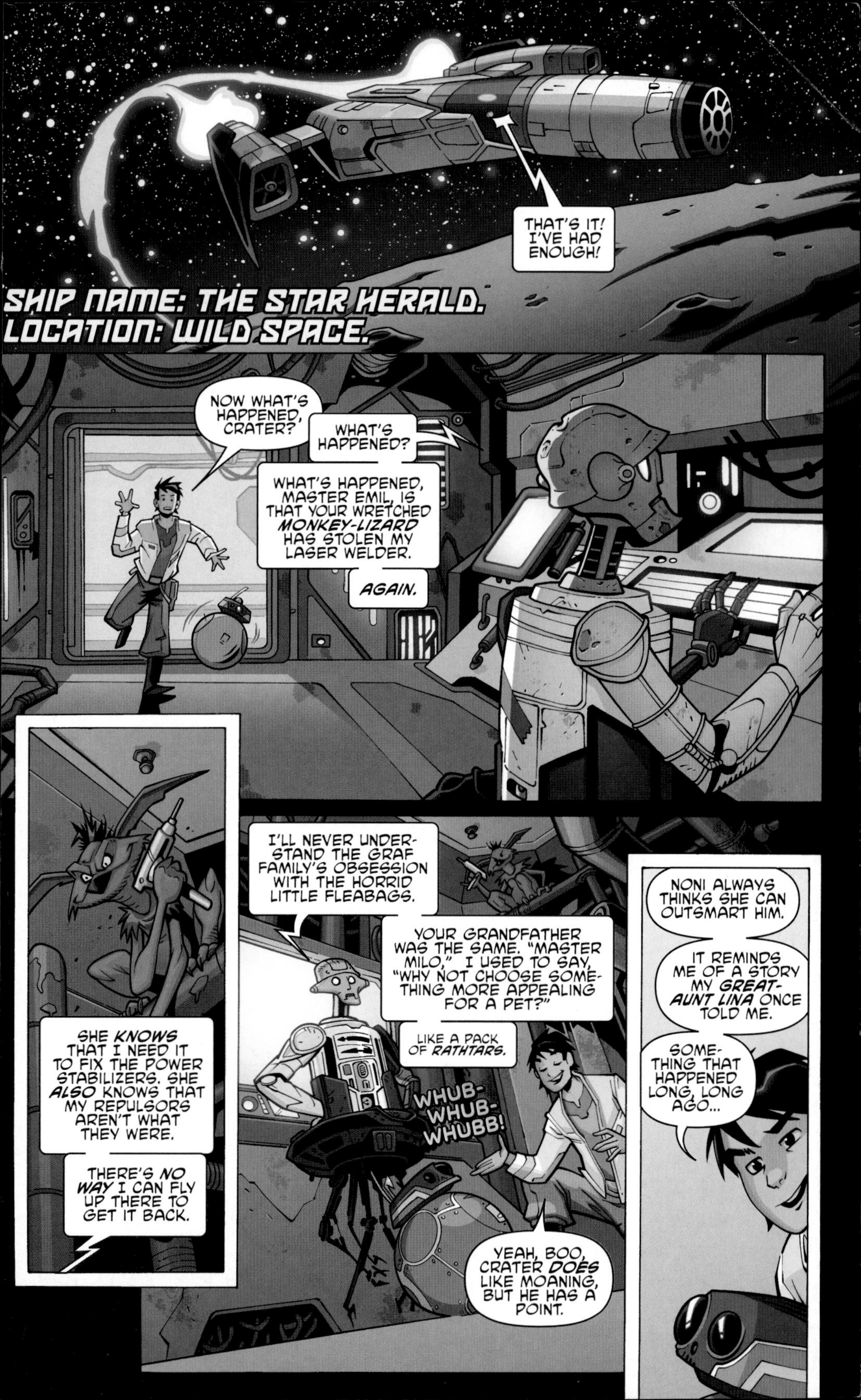
THAT'S IT! I'VE HAD ENOUGH!
SHIP NAME: THE STAR HERALD.
LOCATION: WILD SPACE.
NOW WHAT'S HAPPENED, CRATER?
WHAT'S HAPPENED?
WHAT'S HAPPENED, MASTER EMIL, IS THAT YOUR WRETCHED MONKEY-LIZARD HAS STOLEN MY LASER WELDER.
AGAIN.
SHE KNOWS THAT I NEED IT TO FIX THE POWER STABILIZERS. SHE ALSO KNOWS THAT MY REPULSORS AREN'T WHAT THEY WERE.
THERE'S NO WAY I CAN FLY UP THERE TO GET IT BACK.
I'LL NEVER UNDERSTAND THE GRAF FAMILY'S OBSESSION WITH THE HORRID LITTLE FLEABAGS.
YOUR GRANDFATHER WAS THE SAME. "MASTER MILO," I USED TO SAY, "WHY NOT CHOOSE SOMETHING MORE APPEALING FOR A PET?"
LIKE A PACK OF RATHTARS.
WHUB-WHUB-WHUBB!
YEAH, BOO, CRATER DOES LIKE MOANING, BUT HE HAS A POINT.
NONI ALWAYS THINKS SHE CAN OUTSMART HIM.
IT REMINDS ME OF A STORY MY GREAT-AUNT LINA ONCE TOLD ME.
SOMETHING THAT HAPPENED LONG, LONG AGO...

"...BACK IN THE DAYS OF THE *OLD REPUBLIC.*

"WHEN SHE WAS A LITTLE GIRL, LINA LOVED *DEX'S DINER* ON CORUSCANT. THE BEST *NERFBURGERS* EVER, SHE SAID.

"PEOPLE CAME FROM ALL OVER THE GALAXY TO EAT AT DEX'S.

"*CARTOGRAPHERS,* LIKE MY FAMILY, DOCK WORKERS...

"...EVEN *JEDI KNIGHTS.*

"THE TROUBLE WAS, NOT ALL OF DEX'S CLIENTELE WERE *HONEST...*"

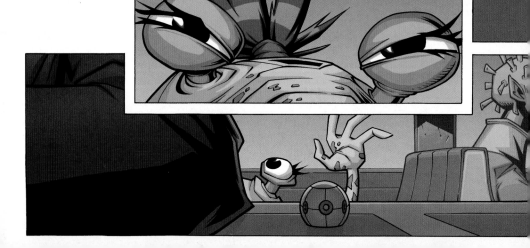

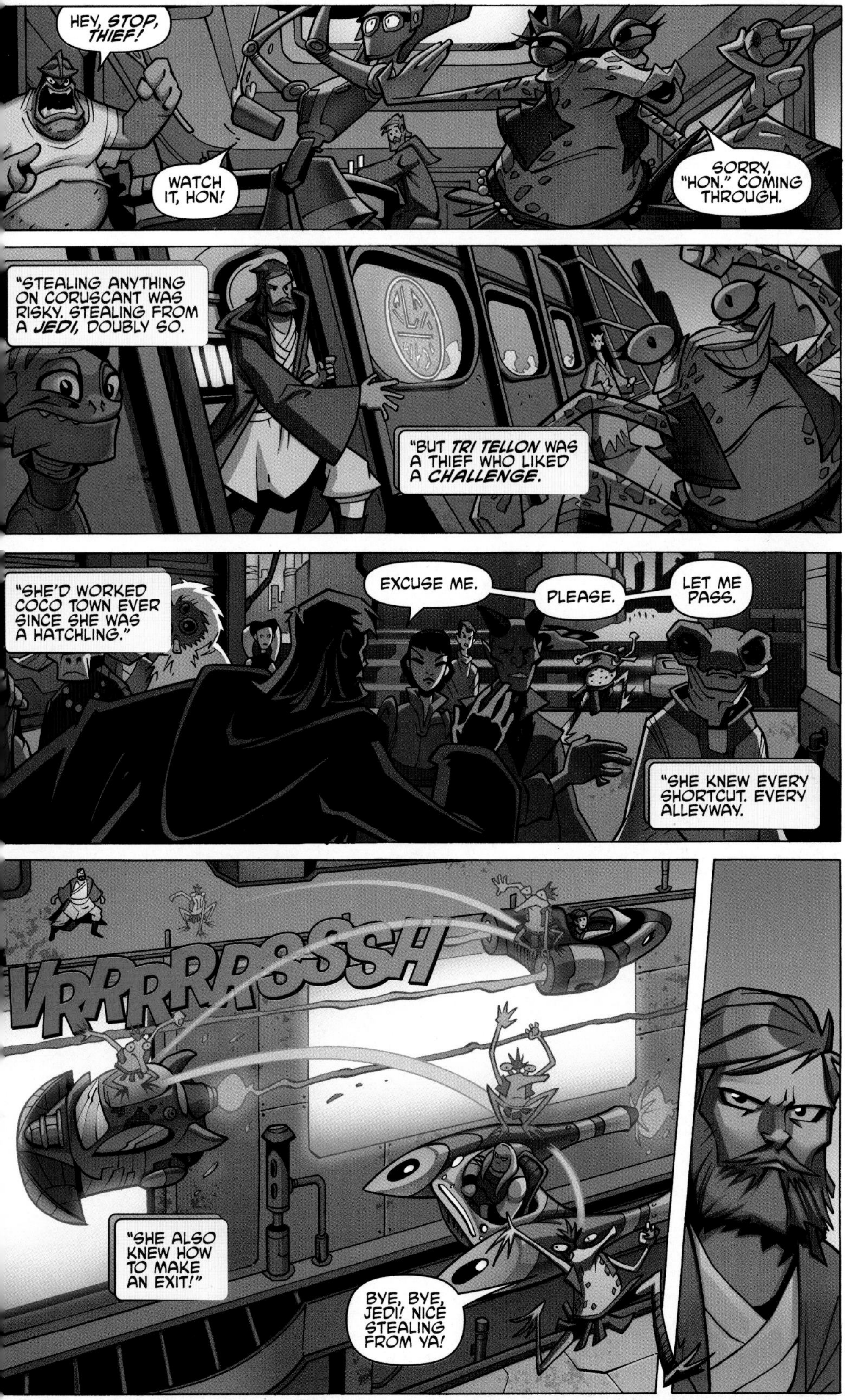
HEY, STOP, THIEF!
WATCH IT, HON!
SORRY, "HON." COMING THROUGH.
"STEALING ANYTHING ON CORUSCANT WAS RISKY. STEALING FROM A JEDI, DOUBLY SO.
"BUT TRI TELLON WAS A THIEF WHO LIKED A CHALLENGE.
"SHE'D WORKED COCO TOWN EVER SINCE SHE WAS A HATCHLING."
EXCUSE ME.
PLEASE.
LET ME PASS.
"SHE KNEW EVERY SHORTCUT. EVERY ALLEYWAY.
VRRRRASSSH
"SHE ALSO KNEW HOW TO MAKE AN EXIT!"
BYE, BYE, JEDI! NICE STEALING FROM YA!

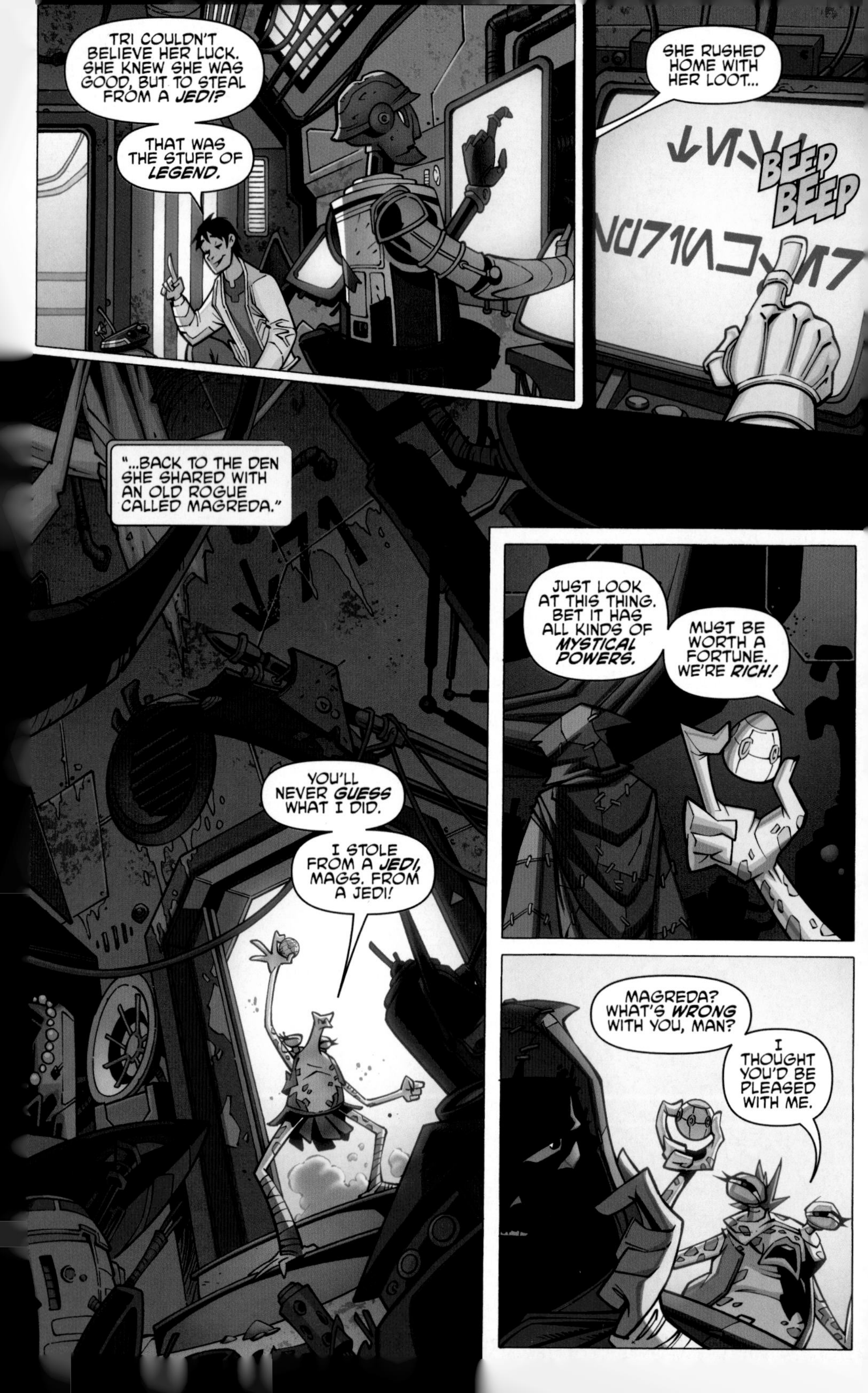
TRI COULDN'T BELIEVE HER LUCK. SHE KNEW SHE WAS GOOD, BUT TO STEAL FROM A *JEDI?*
THAT WAS THE STUFF OF *LEGEND.*
SHE RUSHED HOME WITH HER LOOT...
BEEP BEEP
"...BACK TO THE DEN SHE SHARED WITH AN OLD ROGUE CALLED MAGREDA."
YOU'LL NEVER *GUESS* WHAT I DID.
I STOLE FROM A *JEDI,* MAGS. FROM A JEDI!
JUST LOOK AT THIS THING. BET IT HAS ALL KINDS OF *MYSTICAL POWERS.*
MUST BE WORTH A FORTUNE. WE'RE *RICH!*
MAGREDA? WHAT'S *WRONG* WITH YOU, MAN?
I THOUGHT YOU'D BE PLEASED WITH ME.

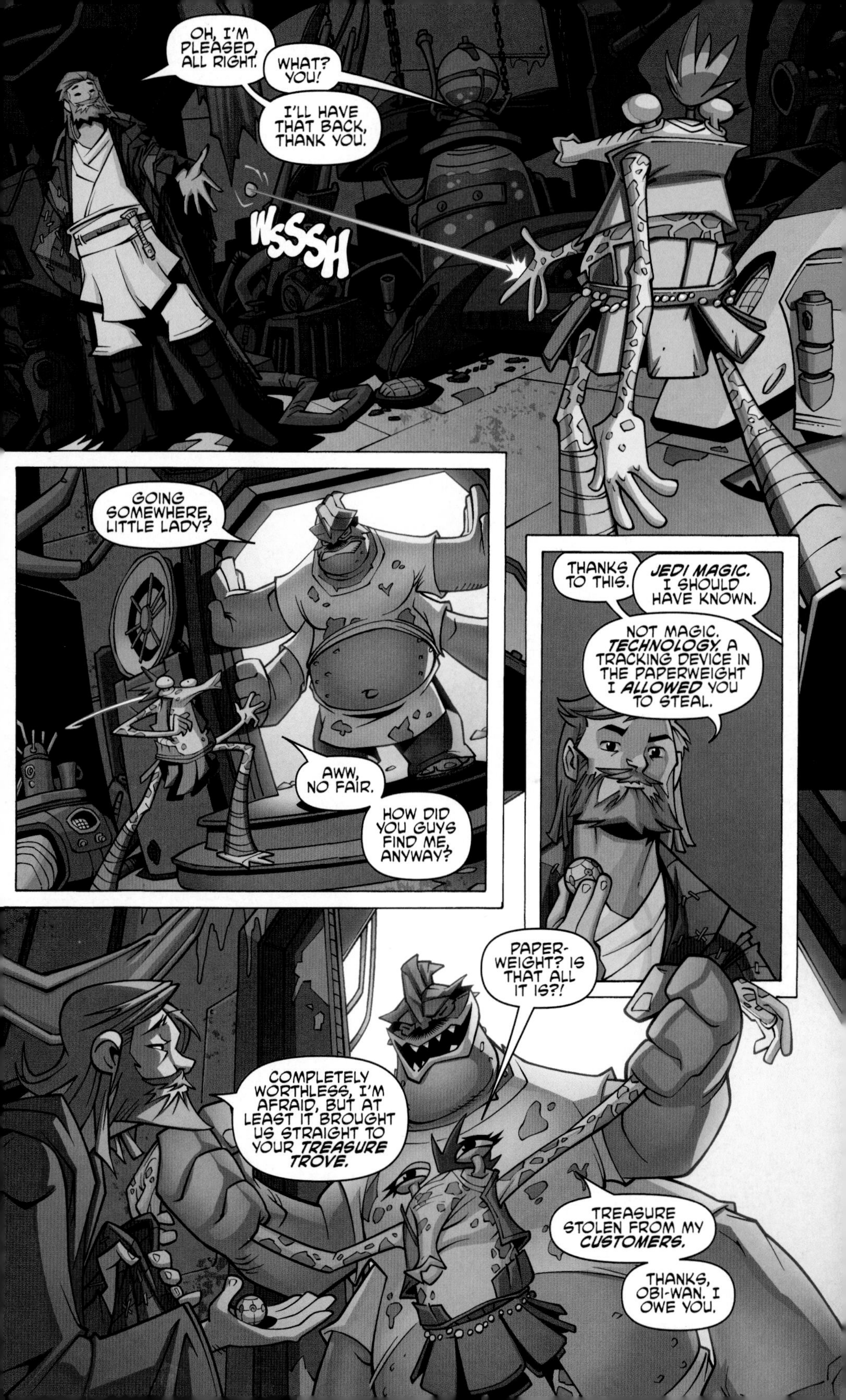
OH, I'M PLEASED, ALL RIGHT.
WHAT? YOU!
I'LL HAVE THAT BACK, THANK YOU.
WSSSH
GOING SOMEWHERE, LITTLE LADY?
AWW, NO FAIR.
HOW DID YOU GUYS FIND ME, ANYWAY?
THANKS TO THIS.
JEDI MAGIC. I SHOULD HAVE KNOWN.
NOT MAGIC. TECHNOLOGY. A TRACKING DEVICE IN THE PAPERWEIGHT I ALLOWED YOU TO STEAL.
PAPER-WEIGHT? IS THAT ALL IT IS?!
COMPLETELY WORTHLESS, I'M AFRAID, BUT AT LEAST IT BROUGHT US STRAIGHT TO YOUR TREASURE TROVE.
TREASURE STOLEN FROM MY CUSTOMERS.
THANKS, OBI-WAN. I OWE YOU.

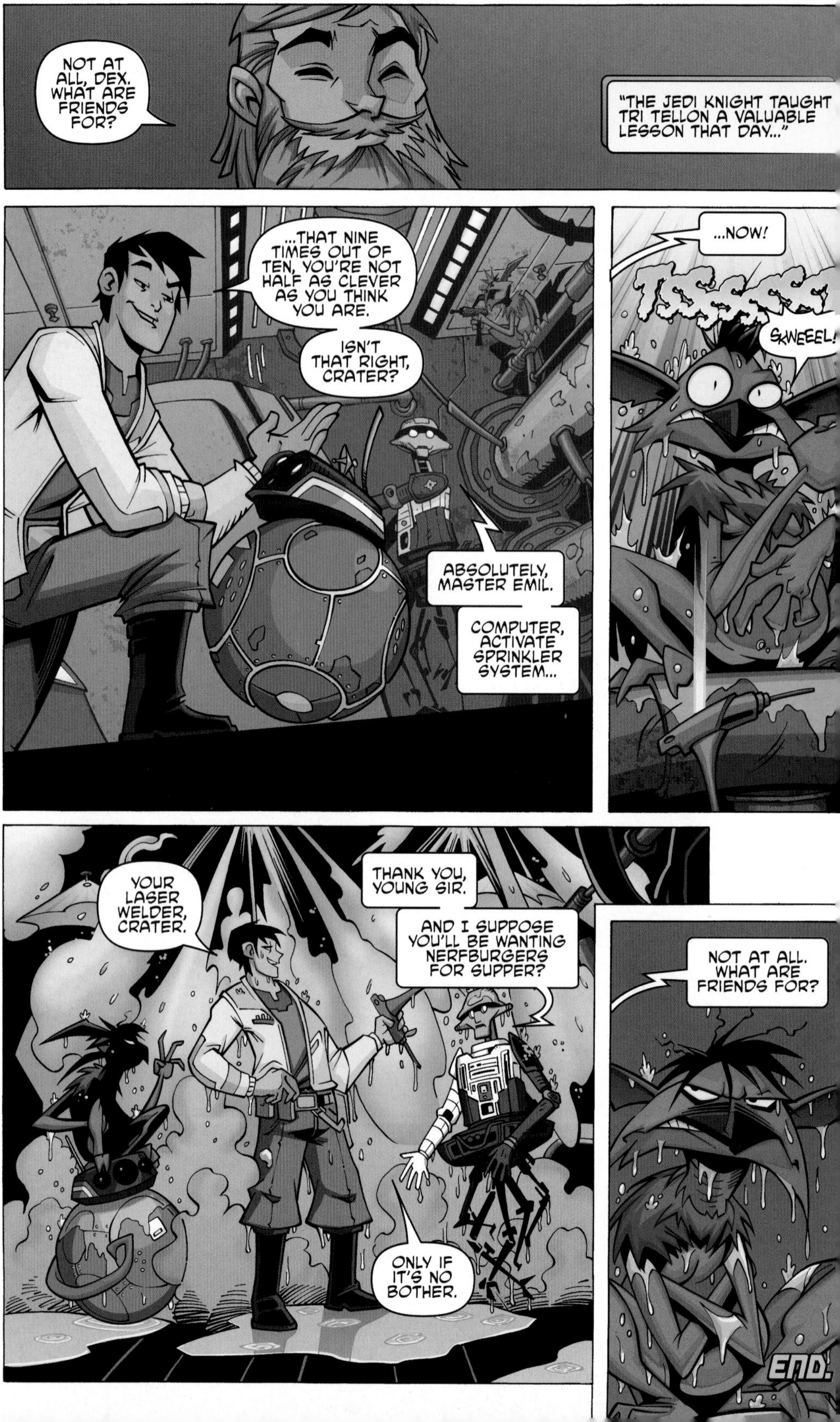
NOT AT ALL, DEX. WHAT ARE FRIENDS FOR?
"THE JEDI KNIGHT TAUGHT TRI TELLON A VALUABLE LESSON THAT DAY..."
...THAT NINE TIMES OUT OF TEN, YOU'RE NOT HALF AS CLEVER AS YOU THINK YOU ARE.
ISN'T THAT RIGHT, CRATER?
ABSOLUTELY, MASTER EMIL.
COMPUTER, ACTIVATE SPRINKLER SYSTEM...
...NOW!
SKWEEEL!
YOUR LASER WELDER, CRATER.
THANK YOU, YOUNG SIR.
AND I SUPPOSE YOU'LL BE WANTING NERFBURGERS FOR SUPPER?
ONLY IF IT'S NO BOTHER.
NOT AT ALL. WHAT ARE FRIENDS FOR?
END.

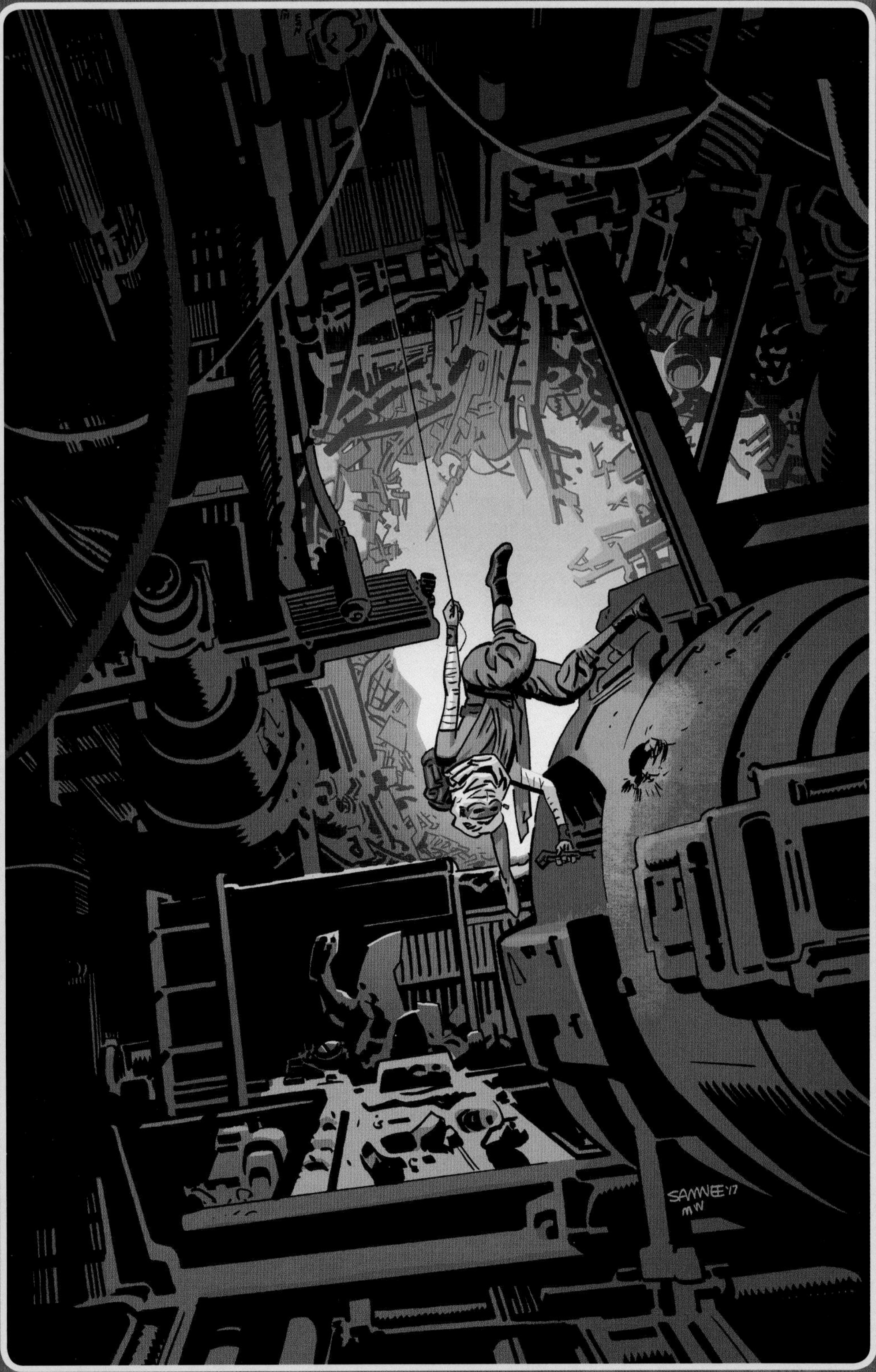
SAMNEE '17
MW
Art by Chris Samnee, Colors by Matt Wilson

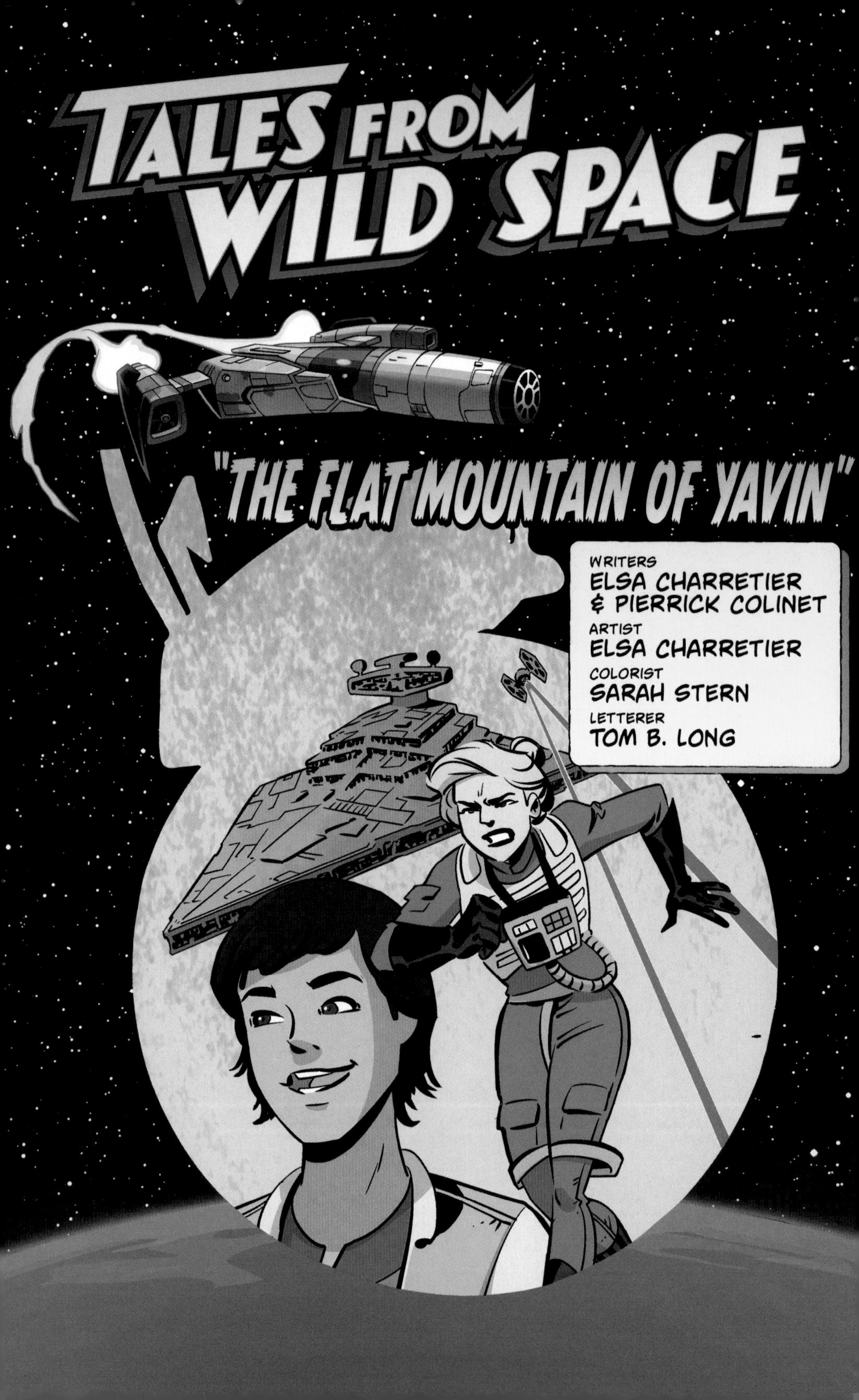

TALES FROM WILD SPACE
"THE FLAT MOUNTAIN OF YAVIN"
WRITERS
ELSA CHARRETIER
& PIERRICK COLINET
ARTIST
ELSA CHARRETIER
COLORIST
SARAH STERN
LETTERER
TOM B. LONG

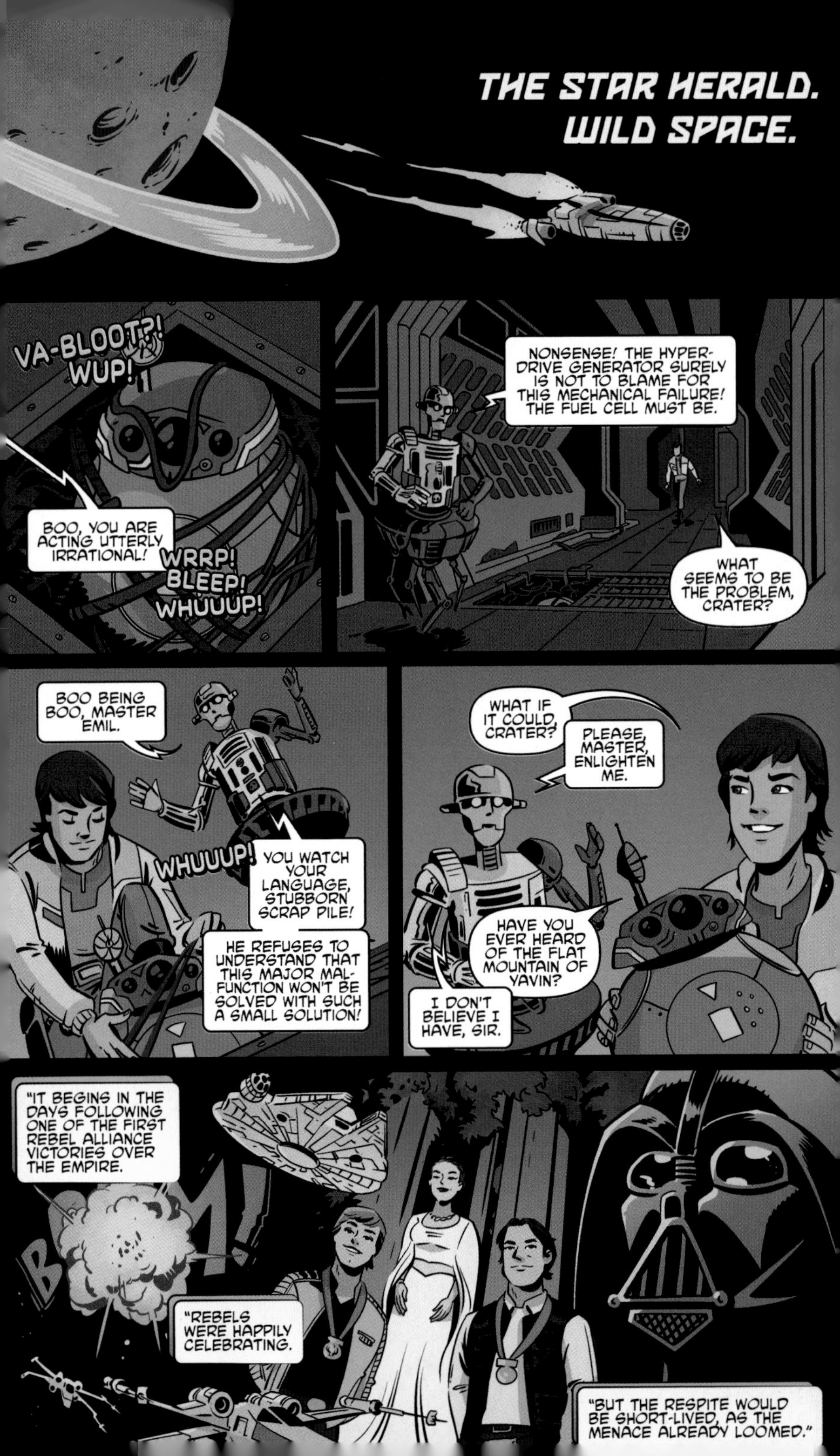
THE STAR HERALD.
WILD SPACE.
VA-BLOOT?! WUP!
BOO, YOU ARE ACTING UTTERLY IRRATIONAL!
WRRP! BLEEP! WHUUUP!
NONSENSE! THE HYPER-DRIVE GENERATOR SURELY IS NOT TO BLAME FOR THIS MECHANICAL FAILURE! THE FUEL CELL MUST BE.
WHAT SEEMS TO BE THE PROBLEM, CRATER?
BOO BEING BOO, MASTER EMIL.
WHUUUP!
YOU WATCH YOUR LANGUAGE, STUBBORN SCRAP PILE!
HE REFUSES TO UNDERSTAND THAT THIS MAJOR MAL-FUNCTION WON'T BE SOLVED WITH SUCH A SMALL SOLUTION!
WHAT IF IT COULD, CRATER?
PLEASE, MASTER, ENLIGHTEN ME.
HAVE YOU EVER HEARD OF THE FLAT MOUNTAIN OF YAVIN?
I DON'T BELIEVE I HAVE, SIR.
"IT BEGINS IN THE DAYS FOLLOWING ONE OF THE FIRST REBEL ALLIANCE VICTORIES OVER THE EMPIRE.
"REBELS WERE HAPPILY CELEBRATING.
"BUT THE RESPITE WOULD BE SHORT-LIVED, AS THE MENACE ALREADY LOOMED."

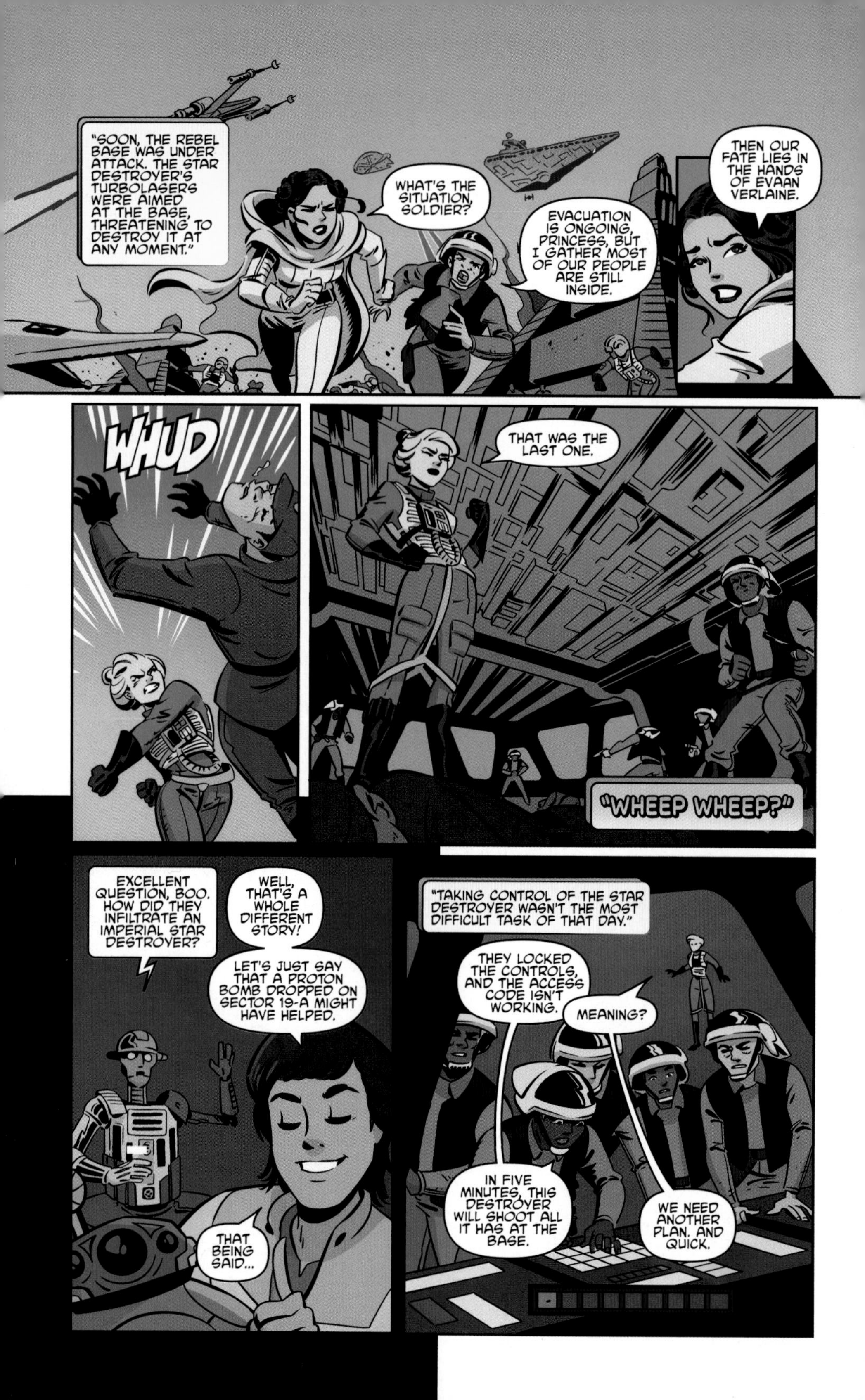

"SOON, THE REBEL BASE WAS UNDER ATTACK. THE STAR DESTROYER'S TURBOLASERS WERE AIMED AT THE BASE, THREATENING TO DESTROY IT AT ANY MOMENT."
WHAT'S THE SITUATION, SOLDIER?
EVACUATION IS ONGOING, PRINCESS, BUT I GATHER MOST OF OUR PEOPLE ARE STILL INSIDE.
THEN OUR FATE LIES IN THE HANDS OF EVAAN VERLAINE.
WHUD
THAT WAS THE LAST ONE.
"WHEEP WHEEP?"
EXCELLENT QUESTION, BOO. HOW DID THEY INFILTRATE AN IMPERIAL STAR DESTROYER?
WELL, THAT'S A WHOLE DIFFERENT STORY!
LET'S JUST SAY THAT A PROTON BOMB DROPPED ON SECTOR 19-A MIGHT HAVE HELPED.
THAT BEING SAID...
"TAKING CONTROL OF THE STAR DESTROYER WASN'T THE MOST DIFFICULT TASK OF THAT DAY."
THEY LOCKED THE CONTROLS, AND THE ACCESS CODE ISN'T WORKING.
MEANING?
IN FIVE MINUTES, THIS DESTROYER WILL SHOOT ALL IT HAS AT THE BASE.
WE NEED ANOTHER PLAN. AND QUICK.

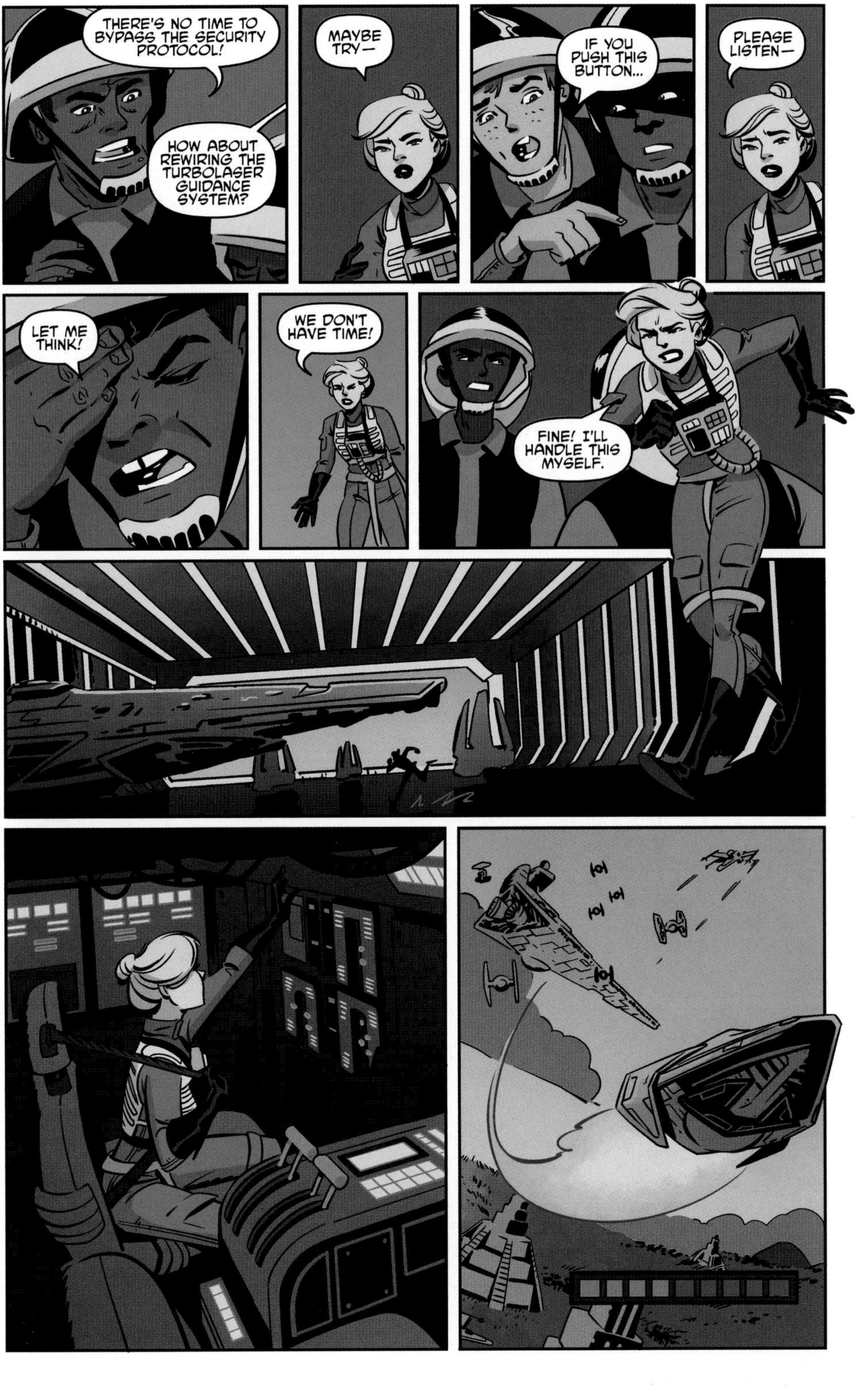
THERE'S NO TIME TO BYPASS THE SECURITY PROTOCOL!
HOW ABOUT REWIRING THE TURBOLASER GUIDANCE SYSTEM?
MAYBE TRY—
IF YOU PUSH THIS BUTTON...
PLEASE LISTEN—
LET ME THINK!
WE DON'T HAVE TIME!
FINE! I'LL HANDLE THIS MYSELF.

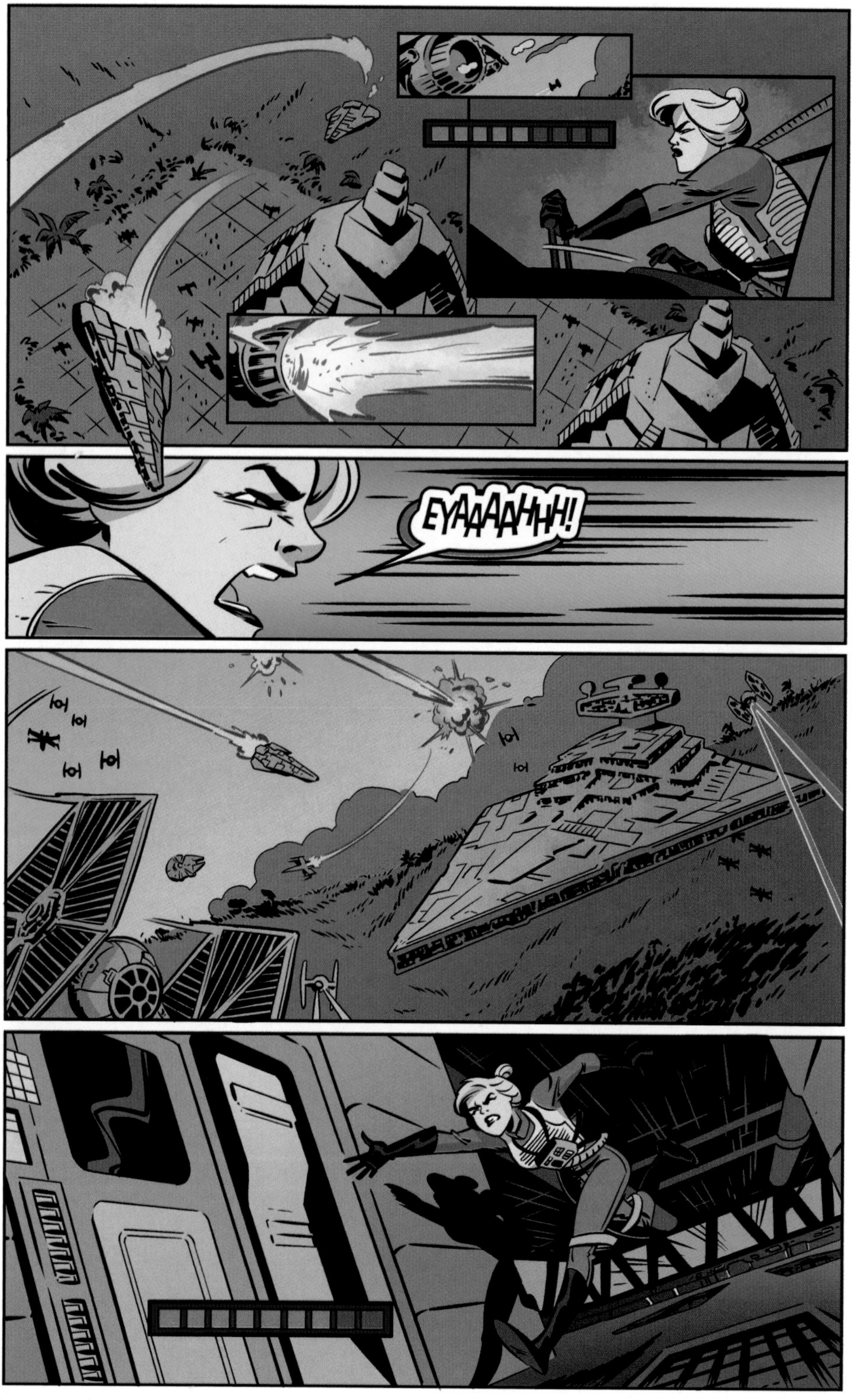
EYAAAAHHH!

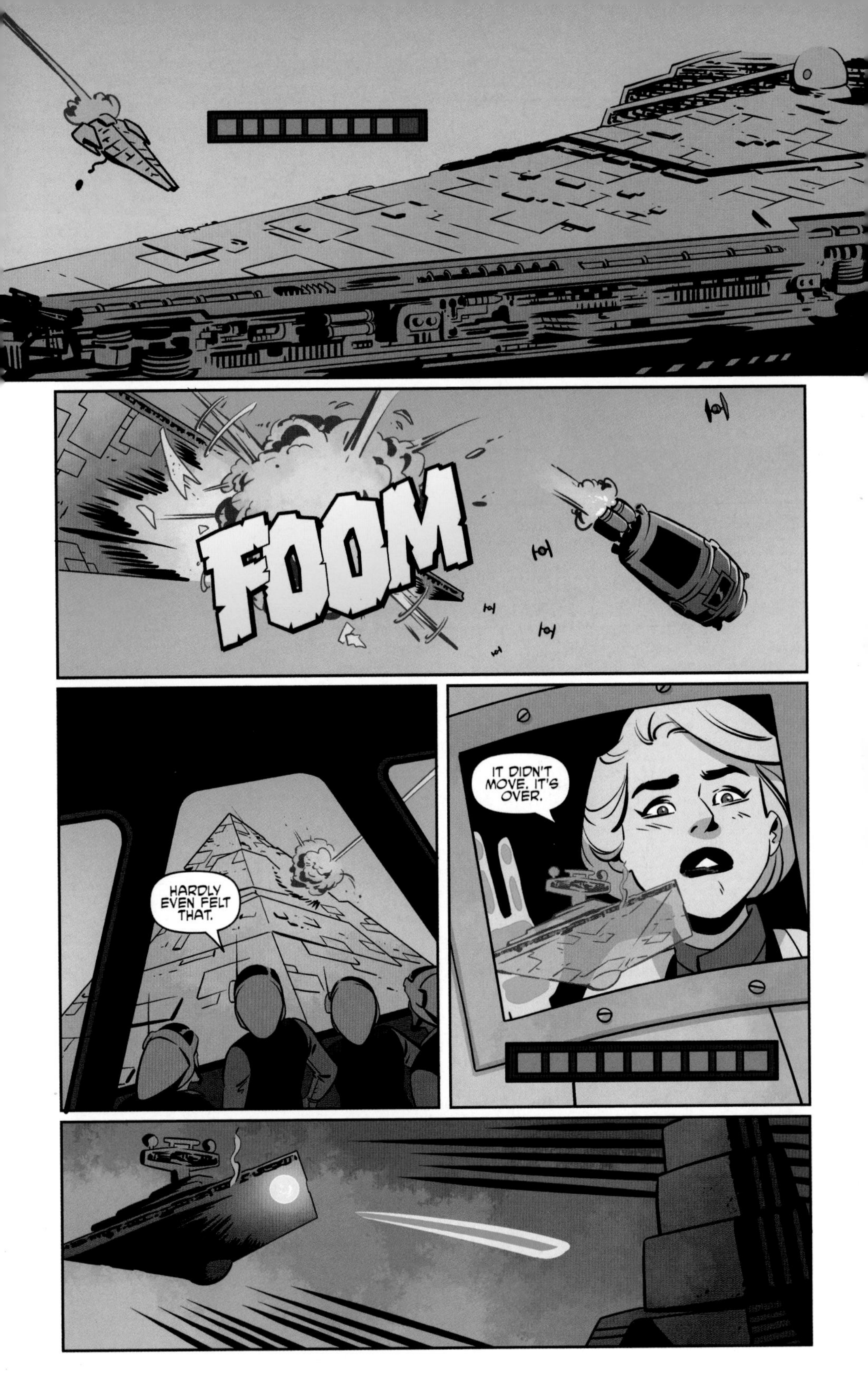
FOOM
HARDLY EVEN FELT THAT.
IT DIDN'T MOVE. IT'S OVER.

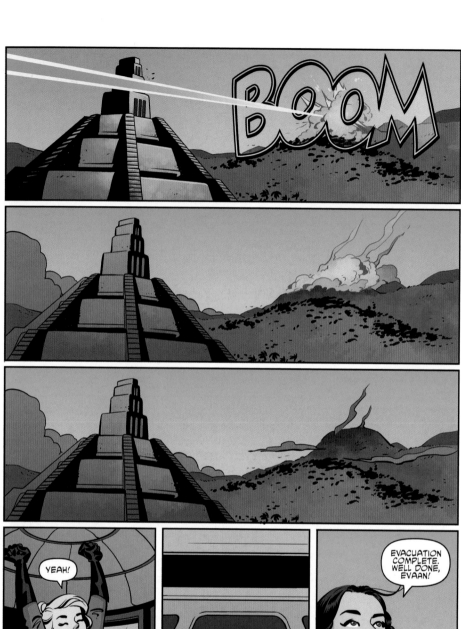

YEAH!

EVACUATION COMPLETE. WELL DONE, EVAAN!

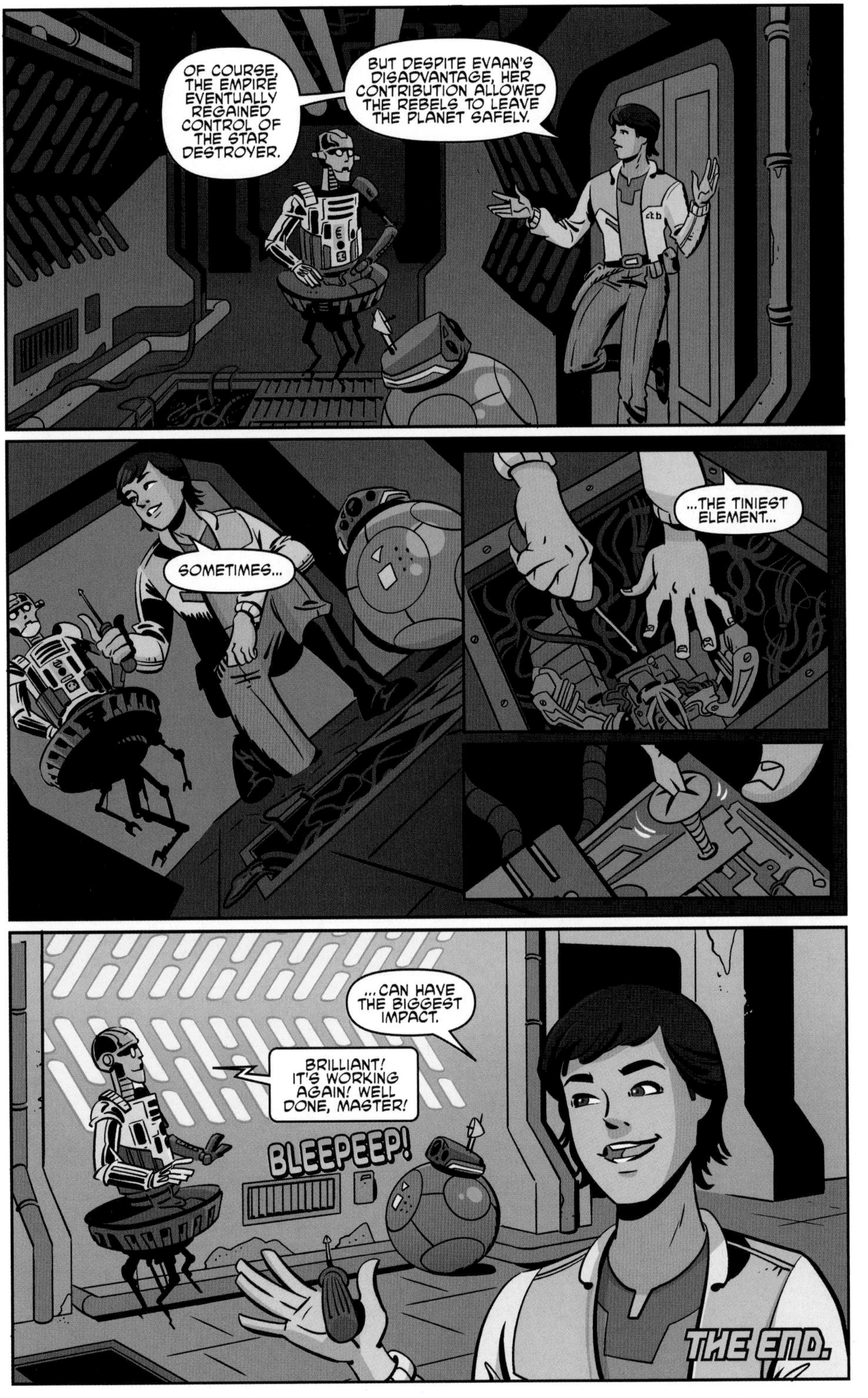
OF COURSE, THE EMPIRE EVENTUALLY REGAINED CONTROL OF THE STAR DESTROYER.
BUT DESPITE EVAAN'S DISADVANTAGE, HER CONTRIBUTION ALLOWED THE REBELS TO LEAVE THE PLANET SAFELY.
SOMETIMES...
...THE TINIEST ELEMENT...
...CAN HAVE THE BIGGEST IMPACT.
BRILLIANT! IT'S WORKING AGAIN! WELL DONE, MASTER!
BLEEPEEP!
THE END.

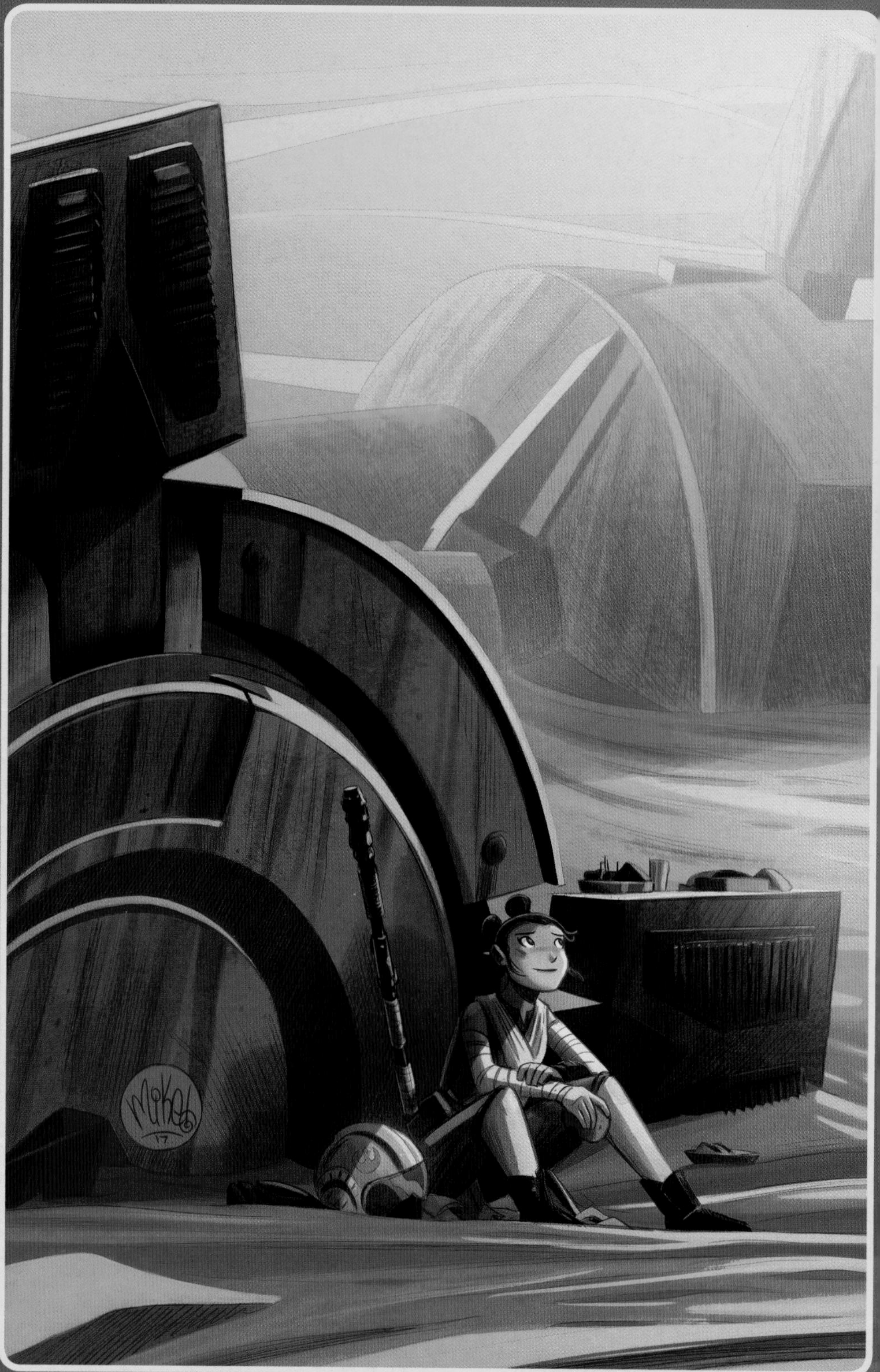

Art by Mike Maihack

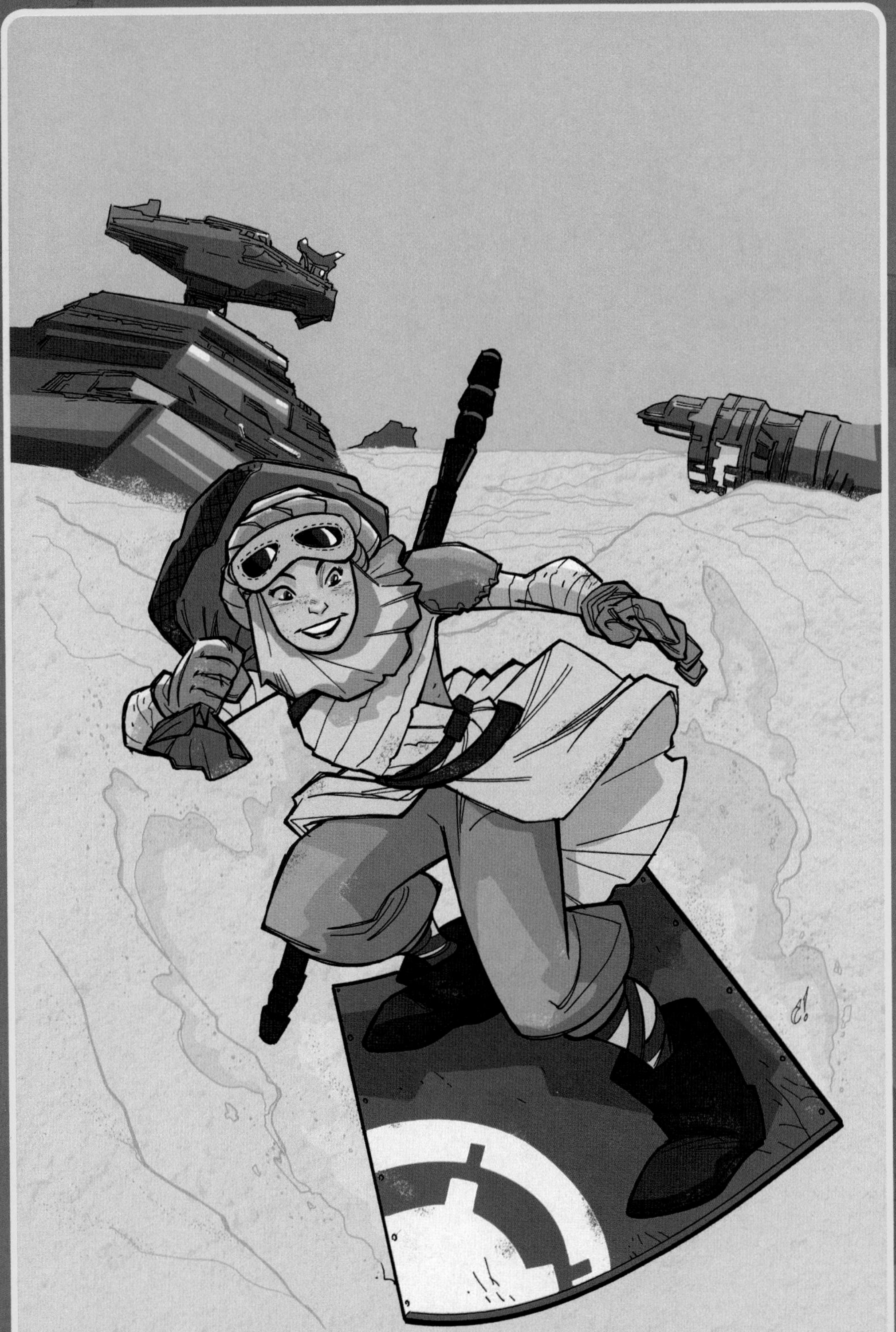

Art by Craig Rousseau

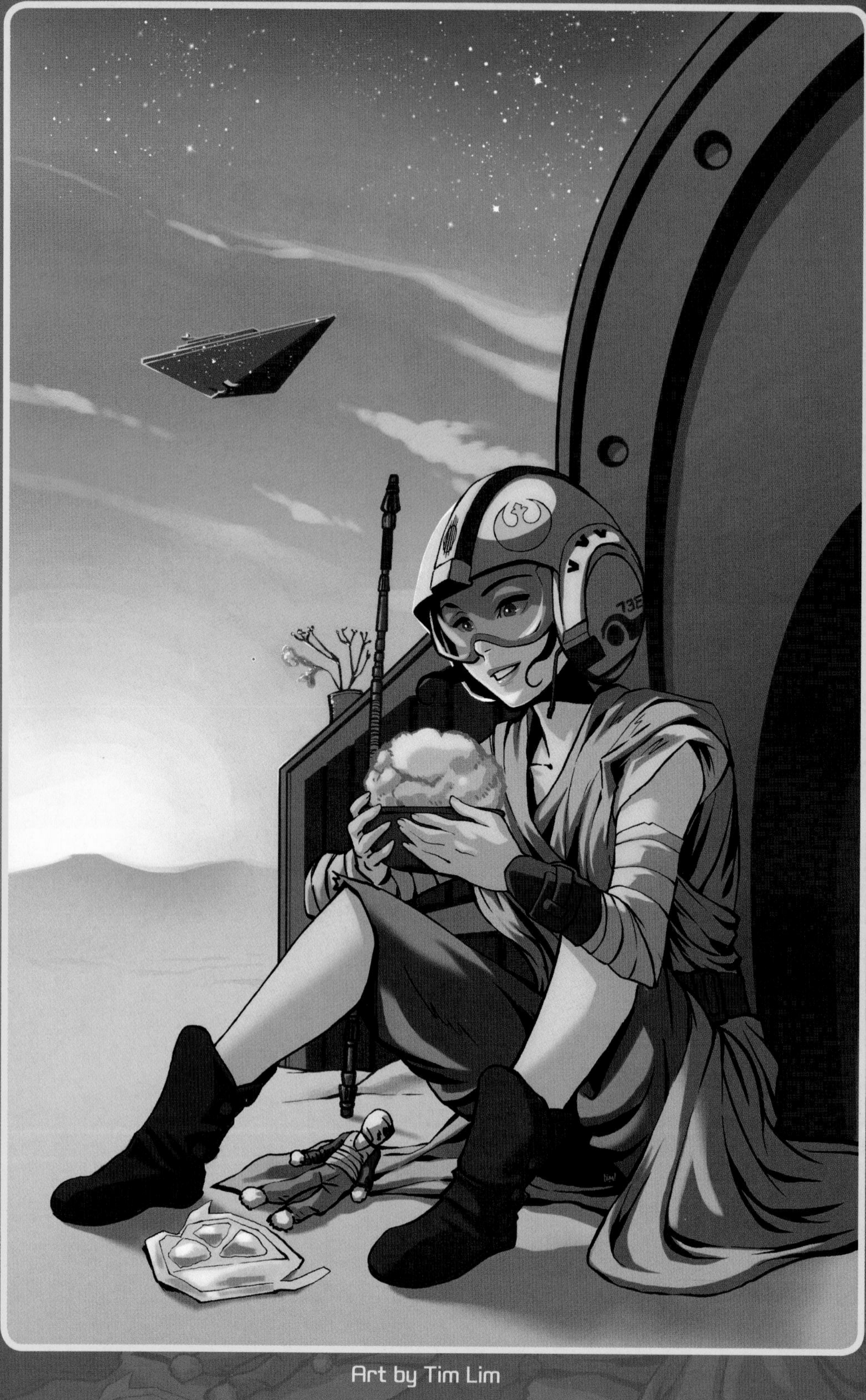

Art by Tim Lim

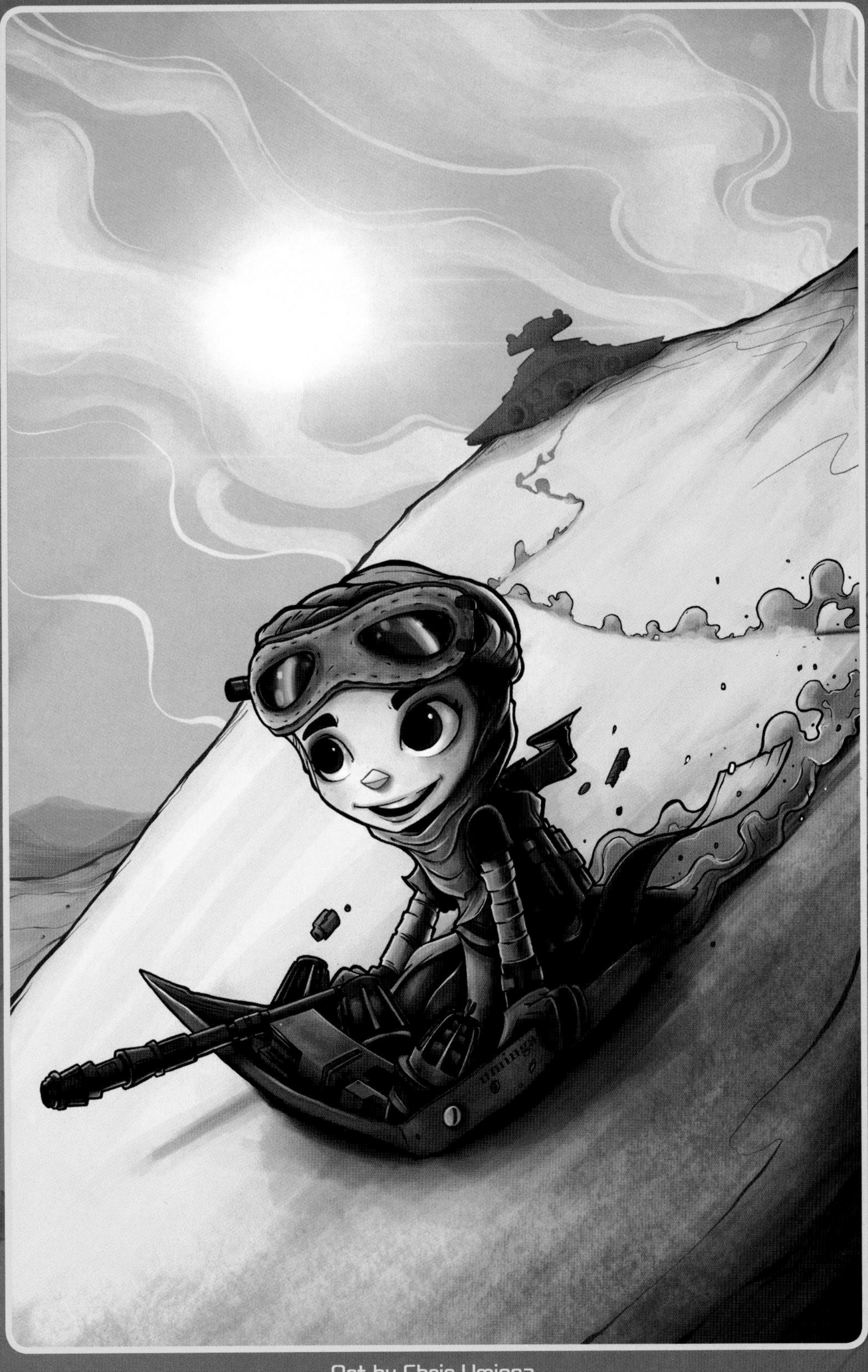

Art by Chris Uminga

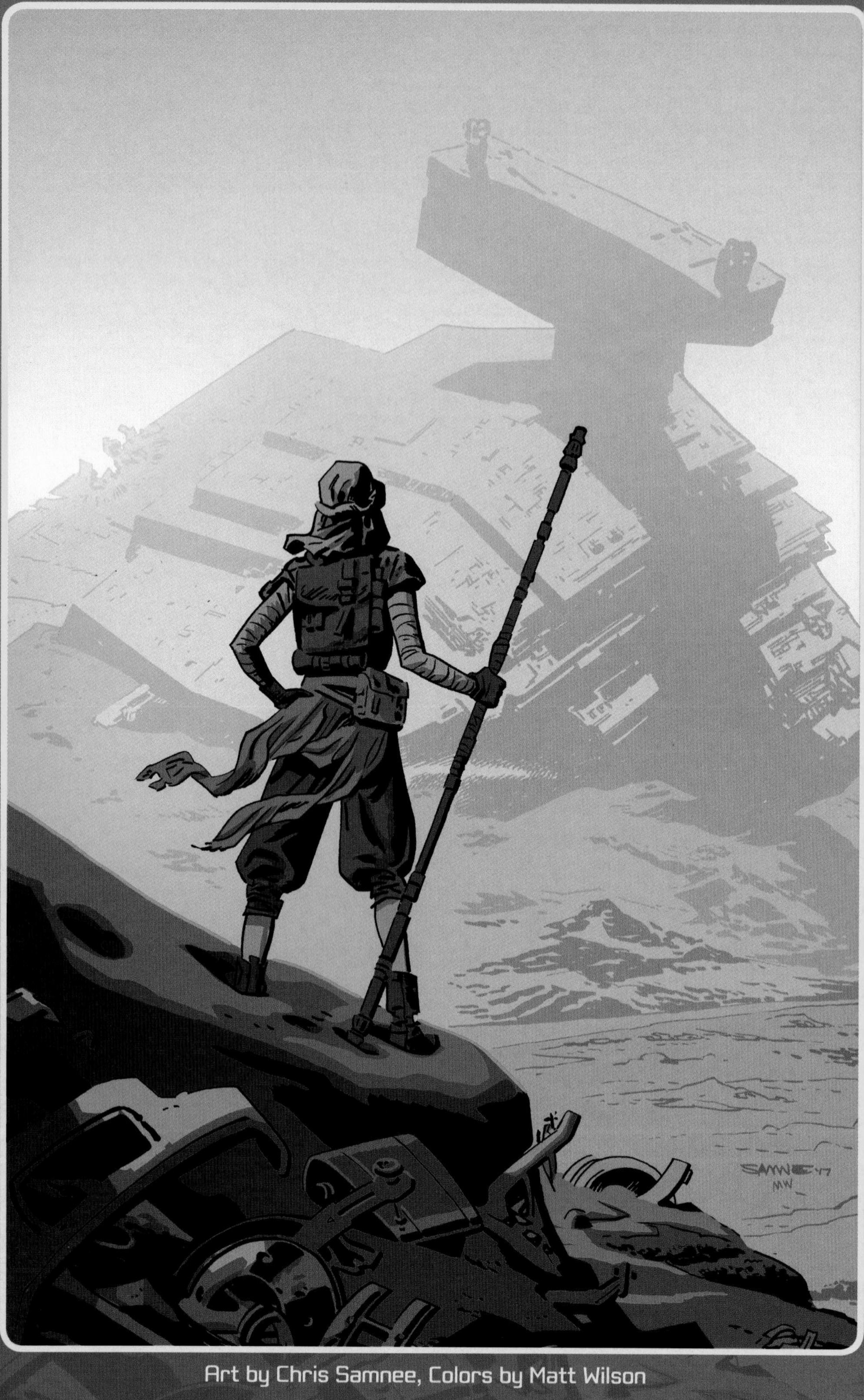

Art by Chris Samnee, Colors by Matt Wilson

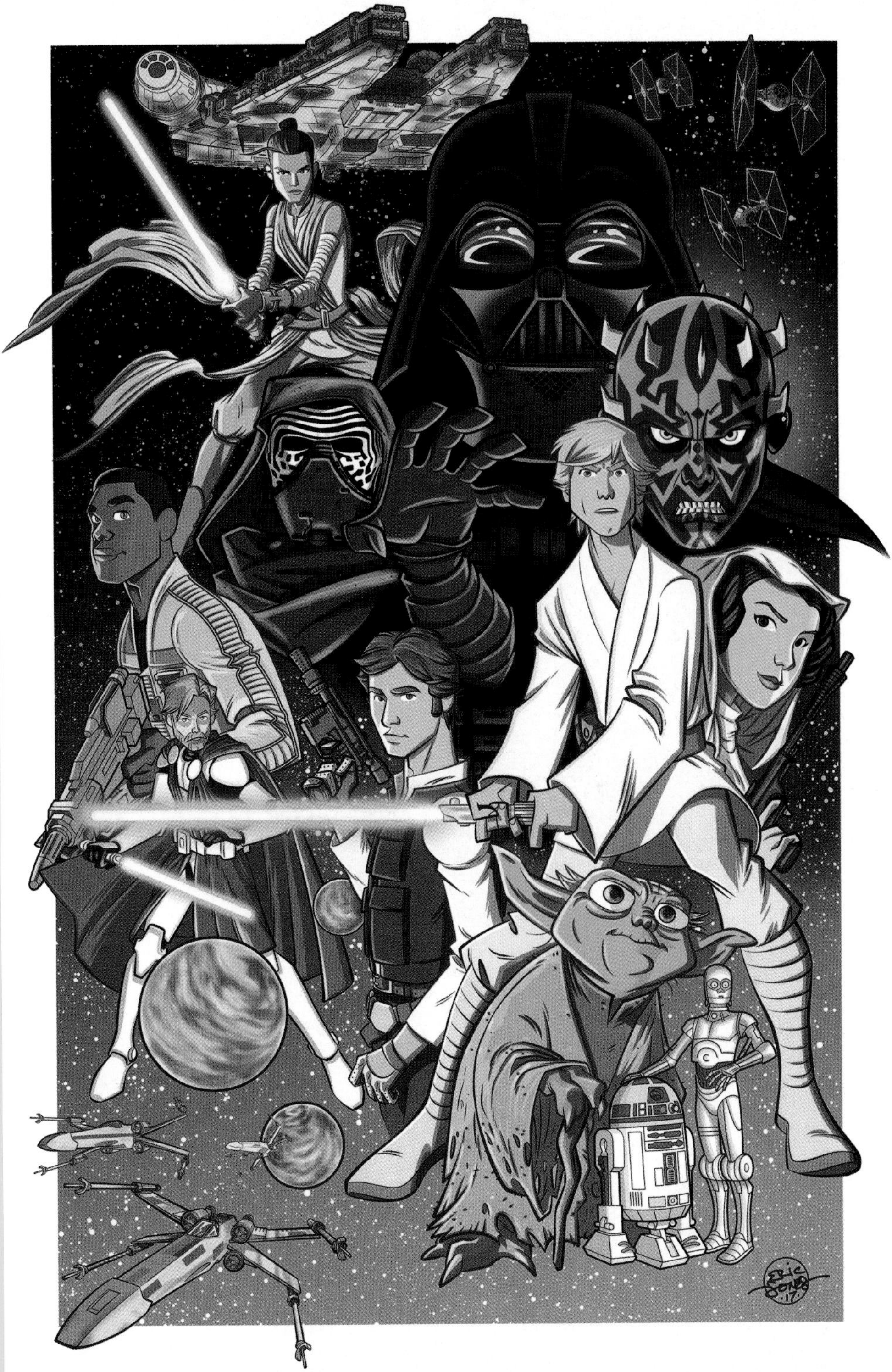
ERIC JONES '17

Art by Eric Jones

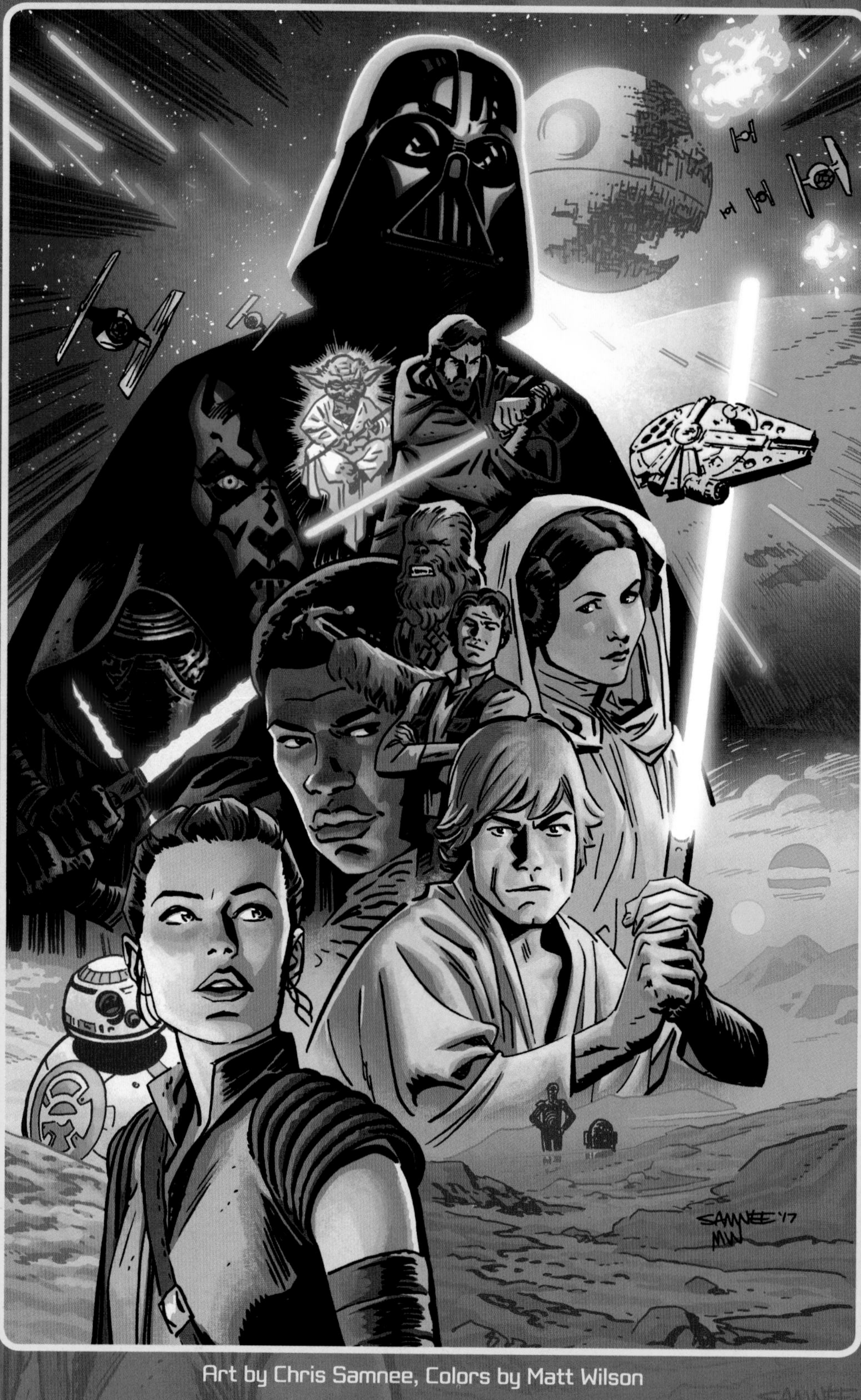
SAMNEE '17
MW

Art by Chris Samnee, Colors by Matt Wilson

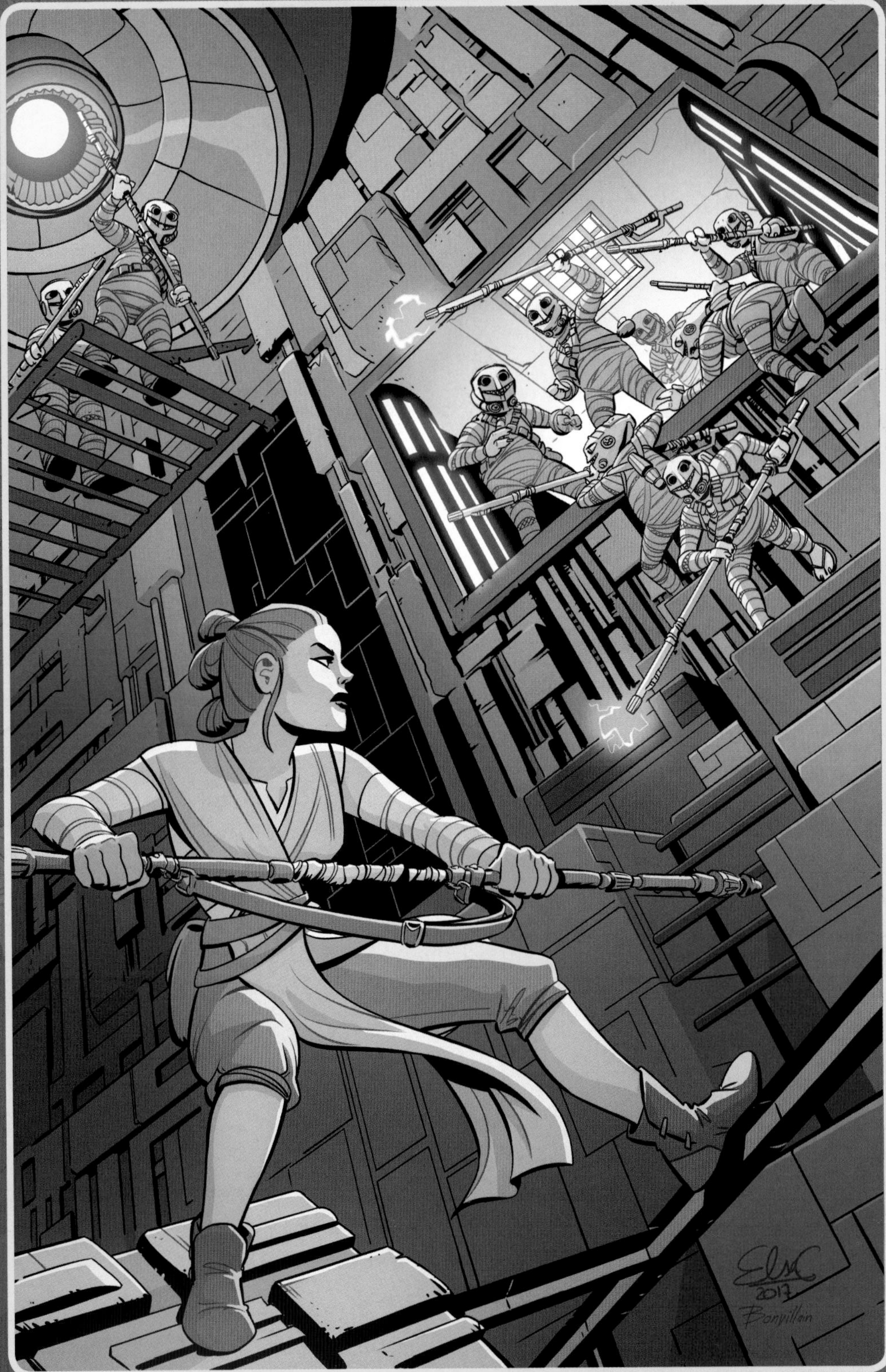
2017
Bonvillain
Art by Elsa Charretier, Colors by Tamra Bonvillain

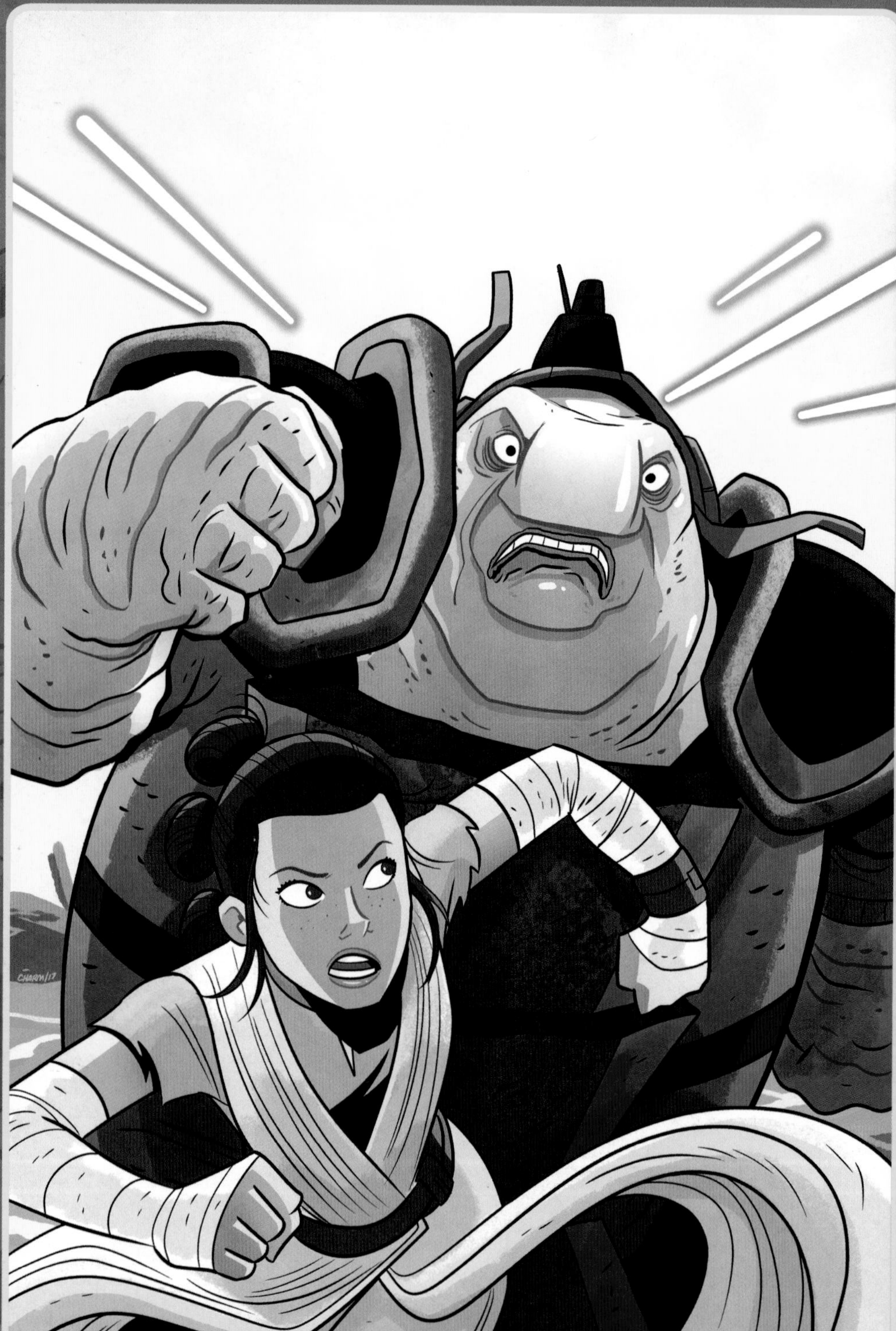
CHARM/17

Art by Derek Charm

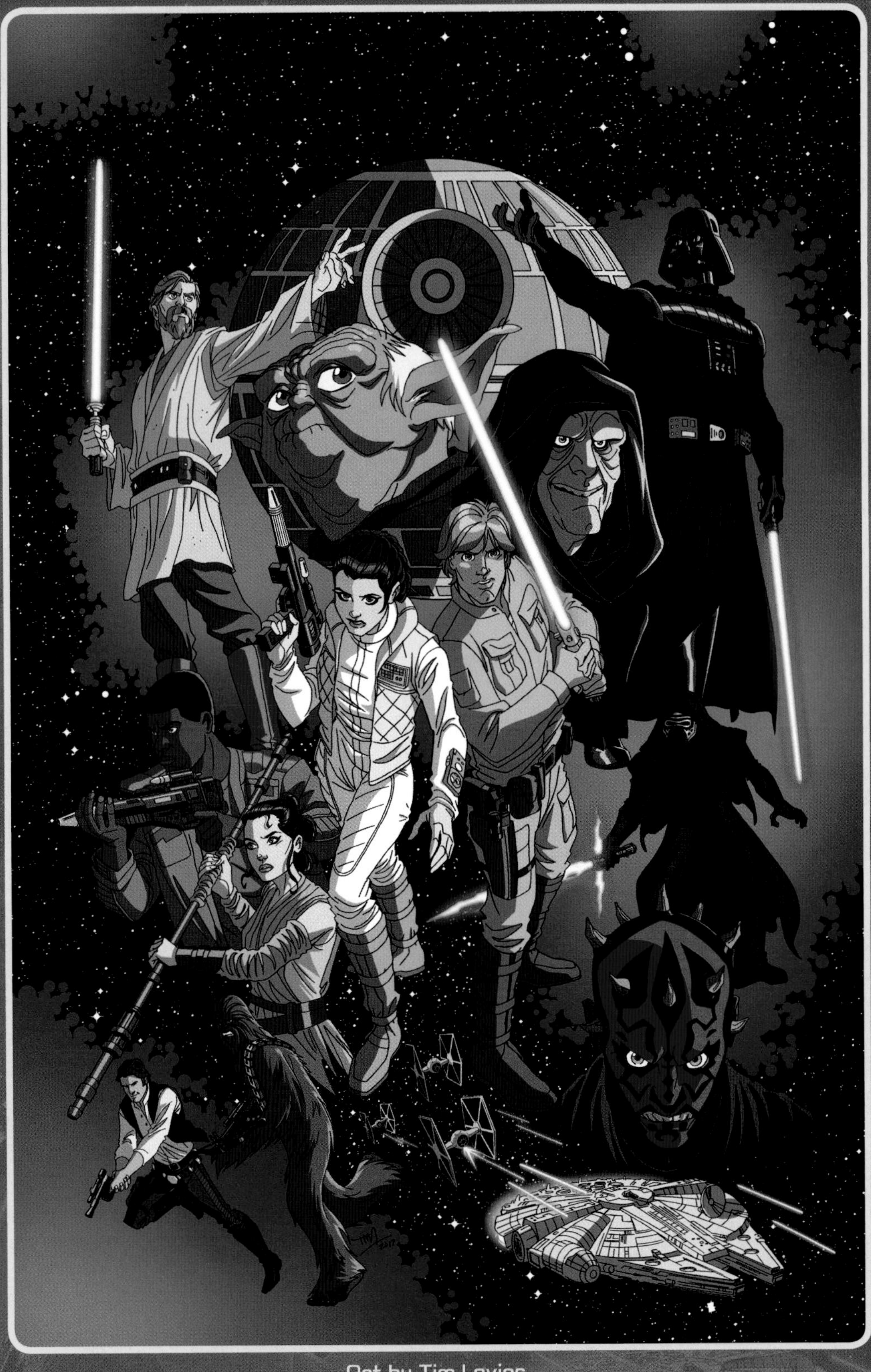

Art by Tim Levins

Character Designs by **Derek Charm**

Constable Zuvio

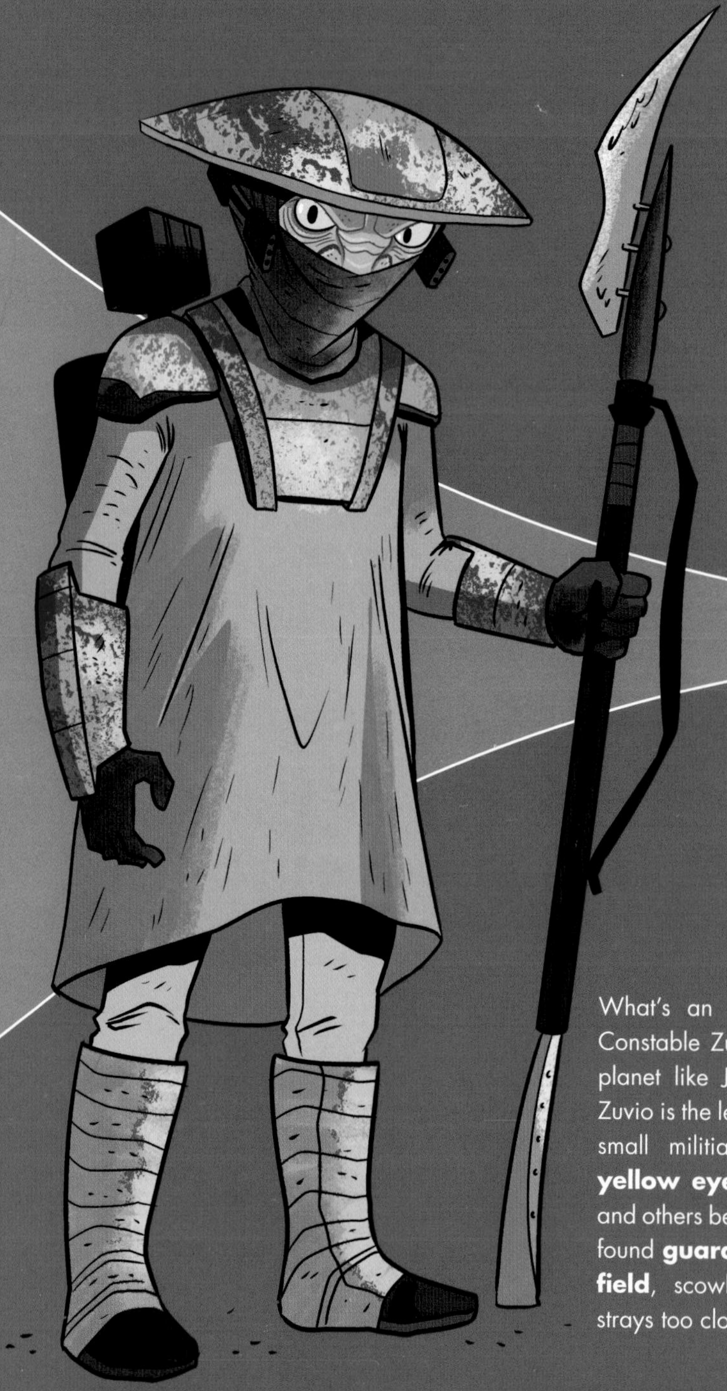

What's an honorable **Kyuzo** like Constable Zuvio doing on a lawless planet like Jakku? The tough, quiet Zuvio is the leader of Niima Outpost's small militia, and keeps a wary **yellow eye** out for cheats, thieves and others bent on trouble. He is often found **guarding Niima's landing field**, scowling at any local who strays too close to a visitor's starship.

Krynodd

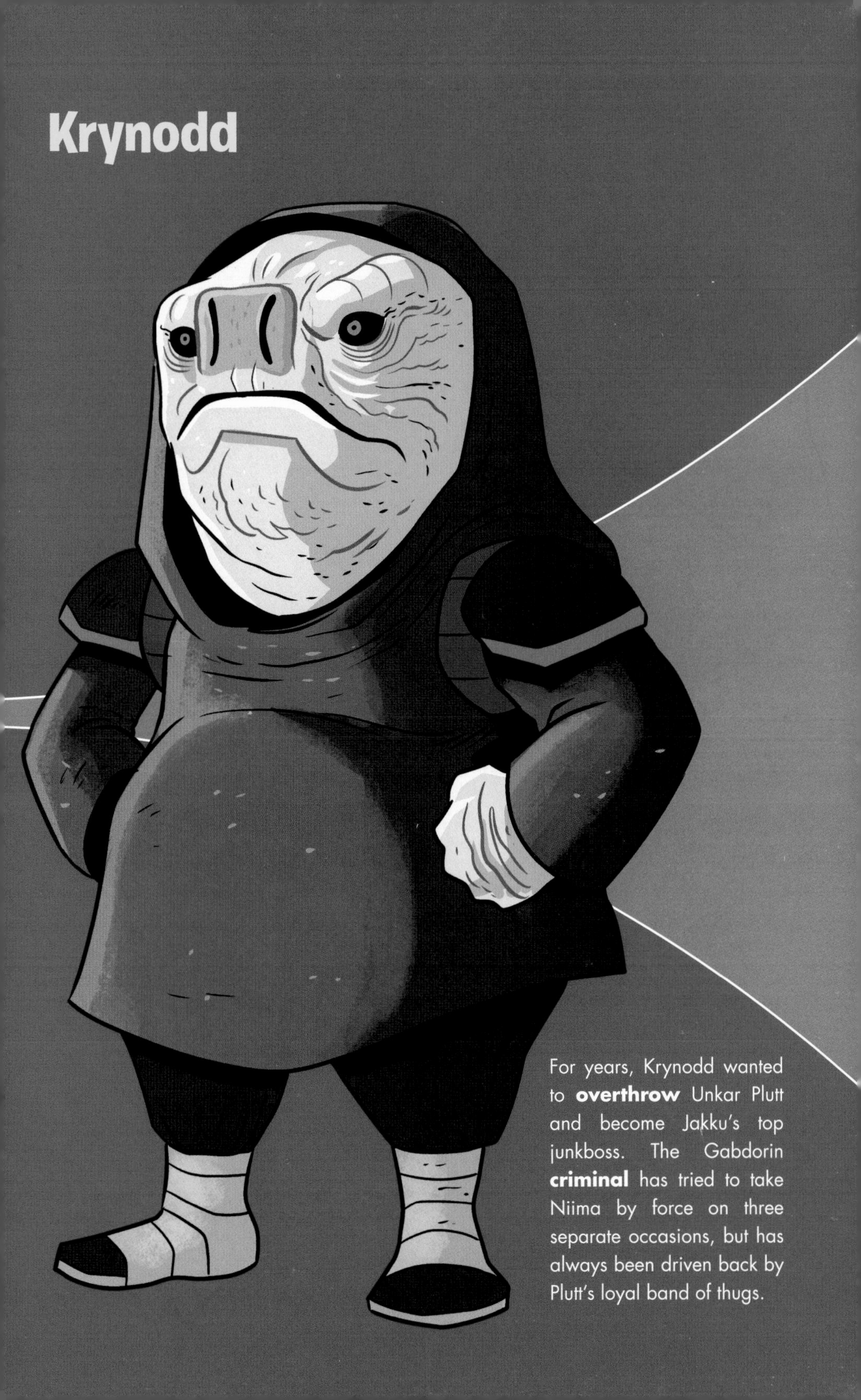

For years, Krynodd wanted to **overthrow** Unkar Plutt and become Jakku's top junkboss. The Gabdorin **criminal** has tried to take Niima by force on three separate occasions, but has always been driven back by Plutt's loyal band of thugs.

Kanna

Don't be fooled by his size. Kanna is a **cunning and creative thief**, constantly updating the Collective's **weaponry**. As a member of the **aquatic Patrolian species**, Kanna has installed a water tank on board Zendiat's ship, the *Fortune*.

Ramakak

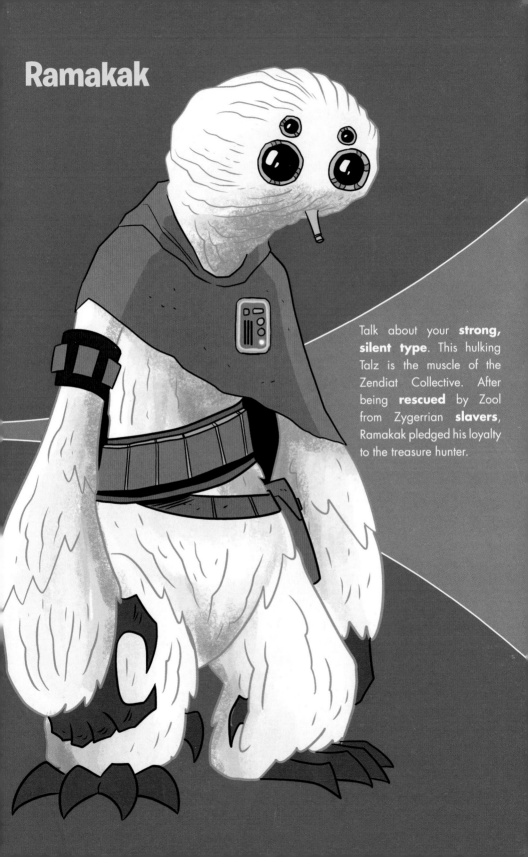

Talk about your **strong, silent type**. This hulking Talz is the muscle of the Zendiat Collective. After being **rescued** by Zool from Zygerrian **slavers**, Ramakak pledged his loyalty to the treasure hunter.

Tryki

A former **Zabrak pirate**, Tryki was **arrested** for attempting to board a First Order cruiser near Rakata Prime. Her ship was destroyed, but she escaped, throwing in her lot with Zool Zendiat.

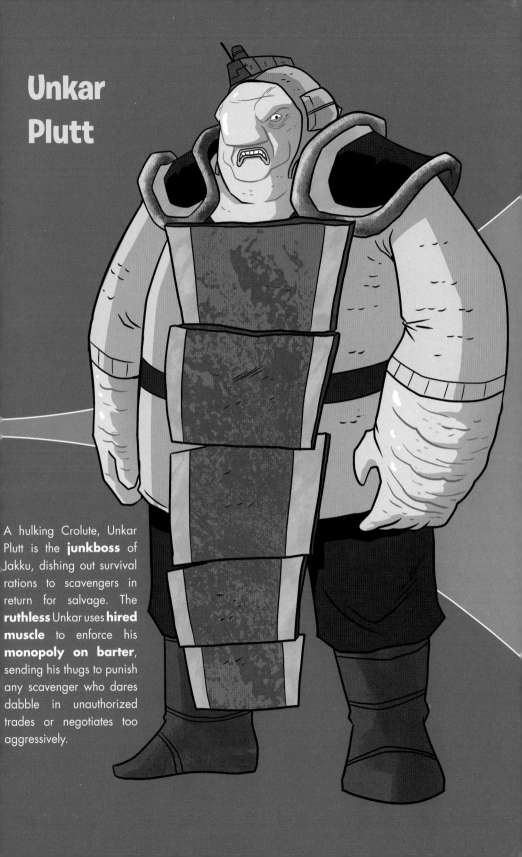

Unkar Plutt

A hulking Crolute, Unkar Plutt is the **junkboss** of Jakku, dishing out survival rations to scavengers in return for salvage. The **ruthless** Unkar uses **hired muscle** to enforce his **monopoly on barter**, sending his thugs to punish any scavenger who dares dabble in unauthorized trades or negotiates too aggressively.

Zool Zendiat

The **ruthless treasure hunter** Zool Zendiat has made a name for himself by stealing **priceless works of art** and selling them to the highest bidder. It is believed that Zendiat was behind the heist to steal Kolka Zteht's famous sandglass sculpture of **Ziro the Hutt** from the **Museum of Tatooine**.

Bobbajo

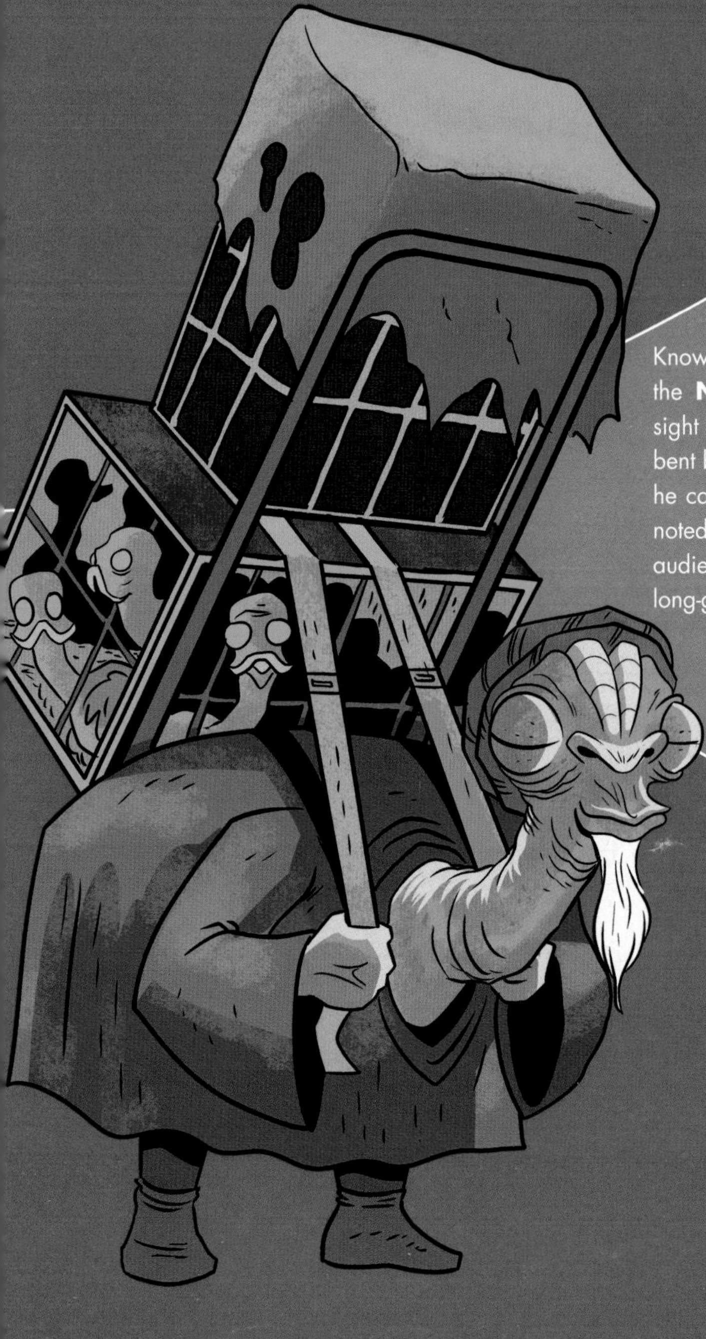

Known as the **Crittermonger**, the **Nu-Cosian** is a common sight in Niima Outpost on Jakku, bent beneath the caged animals he carries on his back. He is a noted **storyteller**, entertaining audiences with adventures from long-gone days.

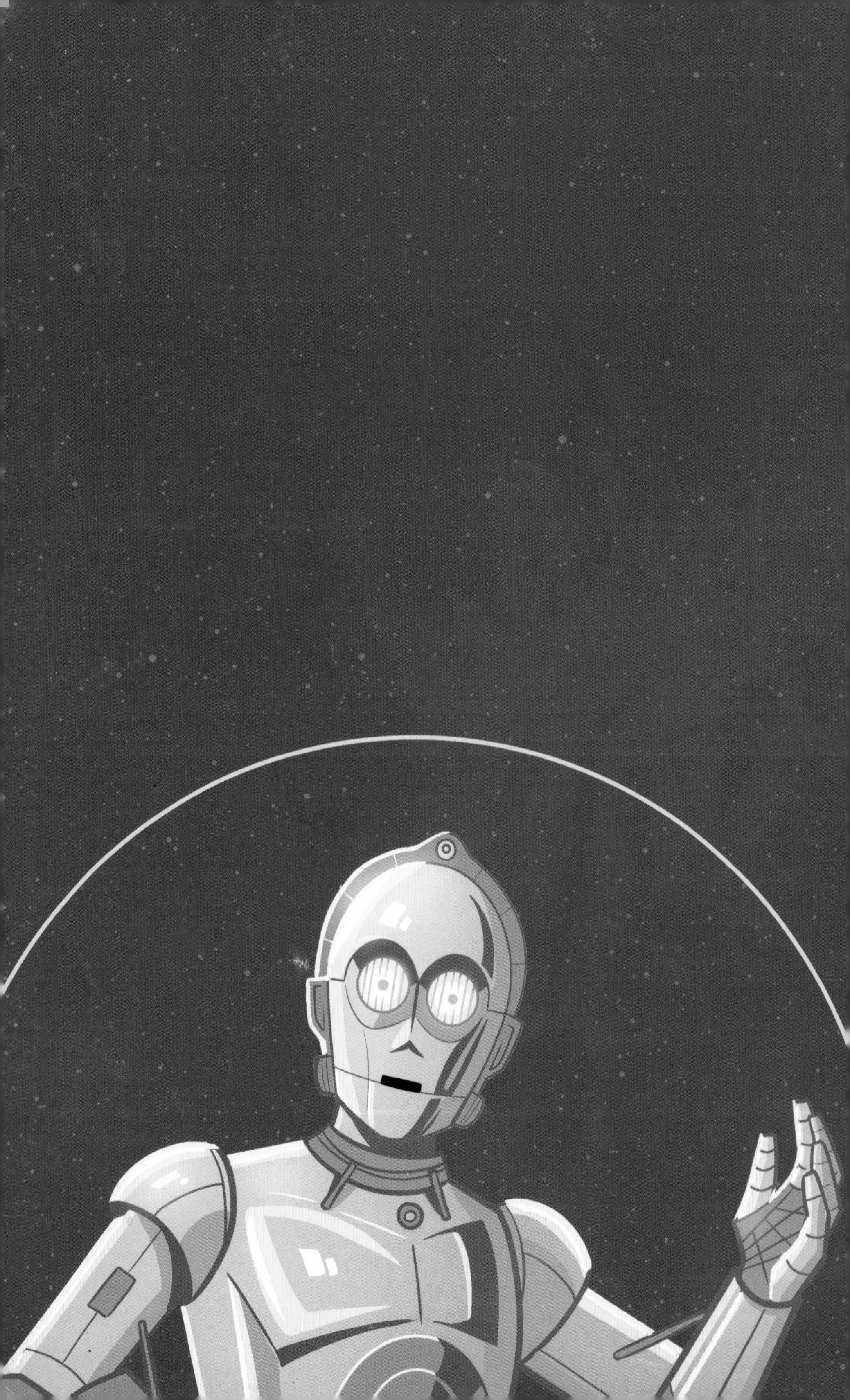